What people are saying about

Three Legs

A moving, funny, and laye... ...the life and mind of a charismatic woman grappling with mental deterioration and the loss of her life-partner. With ruthless honesty and keen observation Moskowitz sympathizes with her characters without ever veering into sentimentality. Readers will root for sharp-witted Sally from start to end and through all the unexpected avenues in between.

Anne McGrath, author, *Best American Essays,* Notable

Full disclosure: I had already read three of Bette Ann Moskowitz's books when I dove into *Three Legs in the Evening*. As an established fan of her distinct humor and sharp-tongued dialogue, I had high expectations, and Moskowitz did not disappoint. Sally is a complex and likeable protagonist who has spent her life as a wordsmith and proud owner of a greeting card shop, comforting her family and customers alike with words of wisdom packed into sleek, memorable phrases meant to soothe, encourage and teach. But post-retirement life and widowhood has her losing her grip and her words as she strives to hold onto her safe and "temperate zone" – eschewing highs and lows – while the world is literally crumbling to ashes after 9/11. Despite insisting, "You can't go east all your life and end up in the west," she does just that – finding pleasure with a new lover, losing her once steadfast control, and walking head-first into the unknown. This is a story of a woman searching for something remarkably different while desperately trying to cling to parts of her past as she begins to cognitively decline. It's about love, aging, bravery, and navigating complicated family ties. It's raw and truthful. You will tear up and laugh out loud. Be sure to allot several hours of quiet time. You won't be able to put this one down.

Myrna Haskell, executive editor of *Sanctuary* magazine

Three Legs
in the Evening

Three Legs
in the Evening

Bette Ann Moskowitz

ROUNDFIRE
BOOKS

Winchester, UK
Washington, USA

JOHN HUNT PUBLISHING

First published by Roundfire Books, 2023
Roundfire Books is an imprint of John Hunt Publishing Ltd., No. 3 East St., Alresford,
Hampshire SO24 9EE, UK
office@jhpbooks.com
www.johnhuntpublishing.com
www.roundfire-books.com

For distributor details and how to order please visit the 'Ordering' section on our website.

ISBN: 978 1 80341 206 1
978 1 80341 207 8 (ebook)
Library of Congress Control Number: 2022934748

A CIP catalogue record for this book is available from the British Library.

Design: Stuart Davies

UK: Printed and bound by CPI Group (UK) Ltd, Croydon, CR0 4YY
Printed in North America by CPI GPS partners

We operate a distinctive and ethical publishing philosophy in
all areas of our business, from our global network of authors to
production and worldwide distribution.

Previous Books

Leaving Barney ISBN978-1-4620-2700-2
Do I Know You? A Family's Journey Through Aging and
Alzheimer's ISBN 1-58979-070-7
The Room at the End of the Hall: An Ombudsman's Notebook
ISBN 978-94-6209-114-6
Finishing Up: On Aging and Ageism. ISBN 978-1-64504-059-0
Reading the Signs ISBN 978-1-64504-156-6

Acknowledgements

My thanks to Judith Summerfield for her steady encouragement and sharp editor's eye.

Thanks to the Hudson Valley Writers Ink for cheering on my early pages.

Love and thanks, as always, to my family: Lynn, Mike, Mary, Joe, Matt, Rachel, Dan, Danielle, Nick, Jillian, and Olivia.

And to Spencer Gale, whose advocacy in this project and others has made all the difference. I will be forever grateful.

For Marvin, with love

What walks on four legs in the morning, two legs in the afternoon,
and three legs in the evening?
Sophocles, *Oedipus the King*

Prologue

I think about Grandma Sally a lot. Sometimes I channel her. Like when the twins didn't want to wear their Covid masks, I told them the masks were their "secret keepers" and if they put them on they could whisper all their secrets and no one would know. I'm not even sure if they knew what secrets were, but now I can hardly get them to take the masks off. That was something Grandma Sally would have done. And when my older boy asked me what 9/11 was, I remembered Grandma Sally telling me that as big as it was when it happened, it would get smaller and smaller until it disappeared and something else would take its place. The "horror du jour" were her words. She said one day there would be people who felt nostalgic for it or even some who didn't know what it was.

She knew this. She knew about time.

She told us the Holocaust was an event, but it was also an idea, and like most ideas, it moved around depending on who was thinking it. Holocaust, Pearl Harbor, Chernobyl, 9/11, Sandy Hook Elementary School Shooting, pandemic, all the same idea. What will come next? And how are we expected to hold them all in our minds at once before we explode? So we forget and move on. Will it be the new routines of climate change – floods, tornadoes, tsunamis – which will bring the misery next, or will it still be the old-fashioned ones, like human folly and human error, and human anger and human fear? According to Grandma Sally, life is one surprise after another and you don't get to choose whether they are good surprises or bad. You just have to be ready when they come.

She said, "Dust Is Dead but Spirit Lives," but she wouldn't tell me what it meant. "Think about it," was all she said.

CJ Battel Graziano

PART I

Morning: Slightly Reborn

Sally went to a funeral on the morning of August 15. That is, Sally Battel. Widow of Arthur Battel, of Bellerose, Queens. Businesswoman and mother of three complicated adults. And she was a bit discombobulated. Not that she was admitting it, but if she were, how could she not be? It was the funeral of Susie goddam Harris, bitch and best friend for forty years. Even when their lives took different paths, even when they hated each other, they somehow managed to share a small but persistent devotion. So close they seemed to be chewing each other's gum, Sally's mother used to say. Spent hundreds of Saturdays shopping for bargains long after they could afford to pay retail, just for the fun of doing it together. "I'll go if you'll go," they said, back and forth.

This day, in honor of Susie, Sally was wearing a sharp red dress, high heeled blister makers, and a small lace hanky pinned to her hair.

Everyone used to call her Susie Q. *The Susie Q is an old dance,* Sally thought. *You shuffle left and right and shake your finger in the air, like you're warning someone of something.*

A lot of people were at the graveside service and all in all, it was a classy job. The rabbi was tall and distinguished looking, with good Italian shoes and aviator sunglasses, and he wore a Mets baseball cap which he switched to a yarmulke whenever he spoke Hebrew. *Nice touch,* Sally thought. Susie would have loved it. At the moment, he had called a time-out on his easy smile and was directing the mourners to form lines alongside the grave to throw long-stemmed roses onto the coffin. It made Sally think of a late-night emcee interrupting the fun and games to mention world peace. It was like a dream. The whole thing had the sharp, hyper-clarity of a dream, with a hint of something off in the ordinariness of the scene, the way dreams are. The light was shimmery.

Next to the roses was a stack of cards for the taking, with a commemorative poem the funeral parlor came up with, which was supposed to be from Susie: "O, do not grieve for me/ for I shall always be/just a glance away/the heartbeat of your day/and all the stars above/will tell you of my love." Were they kidding? That was *not* Susie. As the rabbi did his prayer, Sally fixed the poem in her head: "Now I'm gone/good and dead/ I don't have to get ahead/Never have to shave or wax/ da dum da dum da dum relax/So don't be getting sad and woozy/just hit the spa and think of Susie." *There you go, Susie Q,* she thought.

The day began cool enough but now it was hot, and the red wool dress with shiny black buttons that looked like licorice gumdrops was drenched in sweat, her pantyhose was sagging, and the shoes were a disaster. The ground was soft from days of rain, and she had to stay on tiptoe to keep from sinking. Her calves were beginning to cramp. She wobbled and grabbed the man next to her, who probably thought she was thrown off balance by grief. He patted her arm.

The rows of stones and hedges and paths were neat and green. Susie had looked for this burial plot with the same shopaholic gusto she applied to shopping for shoes. Didn't like the scraggly shrubs at one site. Too much foot traffic at another. A plot near the front gate? No good because soot from the road would dirty her headstone. For a while she was leaning toward a drawer in a mausoleum (until Sally started calling it "your final filing cabinet"). But then she found this plot, on a slight rise in the cemeterial flatland. She said, *I'll be buried on a hill,* like she was Scarlett O'Hara and this was Tara. Then she went back to shopping for shoes and waited to get sick and die, so she could look down and lord it over all the other graves.

The first line of mourners, Sally included, were taking turns throwing the roses onto the coffin from the pile next to the grave. The coffin was halfway into the freshly dug hole in the ground, secured by thick ropes, and behind the mourners, the cemetery workers lurked, impatient to get things underway. One of them was smoking; Sally smelled it. It smelled good and she thought *God, I wish I could have a drag*, though she hadn't smoked in years. When the mourners were done, the workers would take over, lower Susie in the box all the way down and cover her up with the mountain of freshly dug earth sitting there, waiting.

Sally couldn't cry. She tossed her rose, thinking of Susie, of one day last year, they were in Bloomingdales, torn between friendship and a size-eight jacket they both wanted. Susie had almost ripped the sleeve out of the jacket pulling it away from her. Later, they had laughed about it. Now, the memory was hers alone. There were a few secrets, too, that she and Susie held between them, big and small. (A teenage miscarriage; how Susie secretly rifled through her husband's pants for spare change and evidence of affairs). Now, each secret was as useless as a single glove.

As Sally was thinking this, she heard a wail somewhere behind her, and a small woman came rushing forward. She stumbled into Sally, knocking her forward, and Sally's heels dug into the soft ground, which then crumbled and gave way, sending her into the open grave, onto the coffin. It sounded like a door slamming shut when she landed, and then she heard a pop and the top button of the red dress rolled off the wooden box and into the pit. The coffin began to creak and sway, and Sally grabbed the thick ropes that held it, and hung on, like she was in a rowboat in a storm. She was calm, mainly because it did not seem to be happening, but rather to be part of the dreamlike day, and something she had been thinking, about times changing and how fast it all goes. She felt a sharp pain in her ankle as she pulled herself onto her knees. Then people began shouting things like "don't move" and "oh my god" and "get help" and "don't touch her" and the voices woke her to the fact that none of it was a dream, and this most unlikely part of it was actually in progress. The rabbi was standing there with his mouth open, his eyes opaque behind his shades, the prayer book to his chest, as if he were about to pray her out of the grave.

In the end, it was the cemetery workers who got a ladder, slid it into the hole, pushed it firmly against the wall of the grave, and then helped her get her footing and climb out, while people shouted instructions and talked excitedly. The sun came out, blazing, like *ta-da,* everyone was abuzz, and Sally thought, *Boy, I'm the life of the funeral.*

The woman who pushed her, a cousin of Susie's, sat sobbing on a beach chair someone had in the trunk of his car. As if *she* were the one pushed into an open grave. Sally declined a chair, and leaned against a tree, wondering where she was going to find another black button shaped like a gumdrop. She couldn't stop laughing. She covered her face so Susie's husband, Brad, who was approaching, would think she was crying.

"You okay?" he said.

She hugged him and said, "Fine," into his shoulder.

"You two," he said, shaking his head, "were some pair."

"We went back a long way, Bradley," she said. "Susie would have gotten a laugh out of me falling in."

He agreed, and Sally had a feeling he was a little jealous, wished he had been the one who went in after her. As if there were some special honor involved. As if Susie had picked her.

The two of them had talked about dying when they were forty, not in any morbid way, but concerning who would get whose items of jewelry.

"If I go first, you can have my diamonds because I don't want any daughter-in-law, if I ever have one, to get them," Susie, with two sons, had said.

"If I go first," Sally had said, "you'll have to make do with all my designer clothes and my grandfather's gold watch. The rest of it is split between the girls." Sally has a son and two daughters. Her older girl would sell the diamonds and the younger would keep her turquoise and silver and wear it.

"I'll go first anyway," Susie had said. "I always do things first."

Which was true, Sally thought.

"She was the adventurous one," she said to Brad. "I'll miss her like crazy." And then she did cry, even if it was mostly from the pain in her ankle.

* * *

Sally Visited an Orthopedist with Emily, her younger daughter. The waiting room was crowded, and they had exhausted all the mother-daughter topics of conversation they could think of but were still waiting. As if she could no longer hold it in, Emily said, "Mom, you know Brad's cousin is saying she never touched you, you just... sort of... jumped in."

"That's ridiculous," Sally said. "Who's she saying it to?"

Emily shrugged. "Barry and Harry," she said, naming Susie's sons. Then she saw her mother's face. "I shouldn't have said anything. Forget I told you."

"You should be," Sally said.

The orthopedist was the age of her children and had freckles across the bridge of his nose. "Totes adorbs," her granddaughter would say. The ex-rays showed a compound fracture of her ankle. He put her in a cast up to her knee and they were now settled in his dimly lit office to go over further instructions. He read them off a little brochure which Sally sensed he had made himself and was proud of. I bet you can hardly wait for someone to break an ankle so you can give them one of these and recite from it, she thought.

Each instruction had a bullet on a glossy blue trifold with yellow italic writing. +Water inside cast can lead to **skin erosion.**

+Beware of **swelling**

+If you feel **extreme hotness** inside the cast, call the doctor immediately. "Whoever reaches a doctor immediately?" she said, and the doctor blushed. "Mom," Emily said, putting her hand on Sally's. "Let's just listen."

+Do not slide **sharp objects** inside the cast.

It was so silly she couldn't resist. "I guess no blowtorches or red ants, either," she said. The doctor sighed and put the brochure aside. In summary, he said, it would be a good idea for her to enlist a family member to help her bathe. She smiled and bobbed her head up and down enthusiastically, as if she would actually be caught dead letting one of her children wash her.

At home, she tried a sponge bath, but almost immediately, water dripped into the cast, and she ended up trying to dry it with a hair dryer, which began to feel extremely hot, so she stopped. Then she wrapped a washcloth around the tail of a comb (all right, yes, a sharp object) and slid it inside the cast to get it dry. "Okay, Doctor Frecklenose, I get the point," she said to the empty bathroom.

The next day, she put a chair in the tub, wrapped her cast in a lawn and leaf bag, wound the bag and packing tape around it multiple times, like she did the fig tree in the yard in winter, and hung it outside the tub.

(When her daughter, Fran, asked how she was bathing, she said, "Fine, no problem-o.")

It wasn't fine. It was awkward. Usually, when washing her private parts, Sally didn't look. But the position she was in, in the shower, on the chair, her legs spread so widely, forced her to see herself. *Oh my god,* she thought: her pubic hair was sparse and gray, and unraveled, like a growing-out perm, her sex sagging like stretched earlobes. She closed her eyes.

She never touched herself, was not tempted, but seeing herself like that, the thought struck her that, strictly speaking, her vagina was pointless. It could just as well fall off for all the good it did. *A vestigial vagina.* And slightly curious now, she reached down and put her fingers to it. Nada. Nothing happened. She was unaroused. Well, no surprise there. She enjoyed sex when it came around, but had never been *avid*. "Oversexed" was the word her mother had used (referring to Susie). Not that Sally *minded* sex. She had never minded it. But sex was Artie's department and she had left it to him, just like she had expected him to take care of filling the car with gasoline and changing the water purifier filter under the sink. When Artie had died, it certainly was not having sex with him that she missed most; and it turned out she had not missed having sex at all, hadn't even thought about it – until now. Because suddenly, at this moment, seeing herself like this, she wondered if she was not living life to the fullest. "Live life to the fullest" was something she told her children and grandchildren to do all the time. Shouldn't she be sure she was doing it herself?

The water turned cold and she got out and dried off, reversing the whole procedure, lastly dragging the chair back to its place in the foyer so the children would not see it and know what she had been up to. Then, exhausted, she went to bed.

The threat of being bathed by her children, the undignified and intrusive shower, the giving in to some dead impulse she didn't even believe in – all of it embarrassed her. And covering it up made her feel weak-willed, like she sometimes felt when she smiled back at some TV host's lame jokes on *Jeopardy*, or opened her mouth when she watched someone else eat soup.

She did not expect to feel so... *hampered*... was the word. But who ever knows how they are going to feel? And how inadequate even the best summaries of an event turn out to be. In stories, broken ankles were trivial, even sometimes comical. Like, *Oh, the summer I broke my ankle*, or *I remember when I was learning to ski* or, *Oopsie, what a klutz!* Ankle breaking was an athlete's accident, or a mis-stepper's accident, and the rueful victim almost had to be brave or make light of it. If you were in a car accident, it was a lucky-it-was-only-an-ankle consolation prize. Is there ever an inkling of the real pain and inconvenience?

Any idea of the actual trauma of fracturing your own bone? No, that was a well-kept secret, subverted to the agreed-upon public face of it. *Well, of course that's the point of words, isn't it?* Sally thought. By summing it up, you can domesticate the trauma, even control it. She should know. Words were her business. She wrote greeting cards; words were her trade. Right now, she could create several perfect phrases that would say it all. "What A Klutz!" "Just Glad it's Nothing Serious." "Ankle Breakers of the World, Unite." "I Didn't See the Curb." "I Slipped on a Wet Noodle." "Hard Cases in Soft Casts." "It Coulda Been Worse."

But, as she was discovering, knowing didn't exactly keep her from feeling the pain.

Artie would have called breaking her ankle a "worst case scenario" because she was on her own, all alone in the house. And she kind of agreed. Maybe this was what she has been waiting for: some crisis, after his death, that would finally bring home to her the actual trauma of the public event known as "widowhood" or the private event of losing Artie, neither of which, up to this point, she could quite grasp, even after five years. People talked about "pain" and all she felt was an amorphous thing called "bad." Do I want to feel worse than I do? People talk about "closure," but she was sure that she should feel worse first, before it was case closed. She was tickled by the tiniest feather of guilt, as if she were being disrespectful to Artie's memory, at fault for finding widowhood so manageable. Why hadn't she suffered more? Was Artie floating around somewhere feeling slighted? Well, he needn't be, she thought. It was just that he had been sick for so long that they had run out the clock on everything, and when he died it was like putting a period at the end of a long sentence.

Once she learned how to bathe herself, managing a broken ankle came down to three facts: one, everything takes longer to do. She has to drag around the kitchen to put together a simple meal. She solved this by ordering takeout every night from a pile of menus from local Italian, Greek, Thai restaurants. Two, there was the problem of getting to work. Her place of business was downtown in the financial district and taking the express bus there and walking the remaining blocks to Maiden Lane, a routine pleasure for as long as she could remember, was out of the question. Three, she gave in to the children's advice and took a few weeks off.

She had been in the process of retiring, anyway, so she told herself it was a sort of trial run, though of course not the way she would have wanted it. She had been planning to back out of her present life the way you leave a party: quietly, letting them party on, not even knowing you'd gone. In her own time.

"Happy Retirement! Time To Start Another Life!"

"I'm done," she had told her kids. "I want out of the action. Nothing I need to sell. Nothing I want to buy. It's time to sit things out."

Emily said it sounded like she was depressed, but Sally didn't think so. It was just that the pleasures she craved now were like photographic negatives: a lack of ailments, an absence of thunder, no more mortgage.

In fact, the day before Susie's funeral, she had finalized the sale of her small greeting card company to National Greetings. She had been on Maiden Lane, a few blocks south of the World Trade Center, in the same place, for thirty-five years, long after the area outgrew little companies like hers. She stayed even though it was clogged with too many people and too much commerce. Out of inertia, Artie used to say, but it wasn't; it was because she loved the old, narrow streets, how they wound into one another so you could lose your way and find it again before you knew you were lost. She loved the deep history of the place. She read somewhere that there was once a smithy right where her little shop stood, and a stream where maidens washed their laundry, giving the street its name. She loved the cobblestones, the churchyards, the waterfront at South Street, the way it held itself just slightly apart from the rest of Manhattan, and refused to compete. Let the rest of the city entertain the world, downtown will remain the very definition of money: Wall Street. But, lovely as it all was, she was ready to let it go.

Or so she had thought until now, here at home, away from the world, with her leg in a plaster cast. Now she was beginning to wonder if she had been too hasty. She missed the noise of commerce. Afternoons at home were proving to be a bit deadly. Sitting around the house made her think too much. What if what Susie's cousin said about the grave incident was somehow true? Even though she knew it wasn't. What if it was? At this point, she couldn't remember what had propelled her into Susie's grave or how she had gotten out. And somehow it got all mixed up with feeling maybe she had sold the business too soon, and that Artie was not resting in peace. Sometimes she felt physically dizzy. Some mornings she woke up and for a second didn't know where she was.

And the children... her third problem was the children. They were much too attentive. The correct word was "intrusive," if you asked her, and even though she appreciated their caring, when they showed up at her door without calling ahead, she felt things were out of control. It was as if they were on a continual spy mission. What did they think she was going to do? How, exactly, were they expecting her to misbehave? Did they think she was going to go dancing? Oh, they were definitely trying out the parental role, something she had noticed with the children of some of her older friends. Well, not me, she thought. She was not even seventy. I'm not there yet. So, she decided if they didn't call ahead, she just wouldn't answer the door. Simple as that. Of course, the frantic calls afterward (which she didn't answer) were a nuisance, but she didn't care. They had to learn. What was that old saying, you can't make an omelet without cracking a few heads?

The situation finally came to a head early one morning. Sally was in the kitchen, in her nightgown, in the midst of counting out the scoops of coffee, when there was a banging on the front door, and by the insistence of it, she knew it was her son, Mark. She stayed still until he stopped, as he soon did, but just as she was about to pour the water into the coffeepot reservoir, she heard a rattling at the kitchen door and saw Mark trying to peek inside, through the curtained-glass panes. She held her breath, her heart pounding now, and hopped back, behind the pantry door, and only half-thinking, backed into the pantry and pulled the door in, the narrow space just enough for her to turn herself around and squeeze against the shelves, and there she hid until she heard quiet and maybe his heels crunching gravel on the retreat. When she tried to come out, the door wouldn't open. She rattled the knob and banged, even though now there was no one on the other side to hear her, she had seen to that. So, was this where she would be found dead? In her ratty nightgown, pressed against the shelves that separate canned from boxed, her cheek dented from the corner of the Cheerio box, her head resting on a bag of Fritos? She kept at it, twisting the knob side to side, up and down, feeling the loose play, hoping the outside doorknob would not fall off, picturing the outside doorknob falling off, picturing one of the kids coming, their surprise at finding her... how? Dead? Unconscious? Which for some reason made her laugh, the sight of them, in their shock. So laughing and shaking, she finally felt the doorknob yield and flinging the door so hard it hit the wall, she fell back into the kitchen, breathing hard, grabbing for stability, blinking in the kitchen light, laughing tears. The phone rang at that moment and because she was still discombobulated, she forgot to not answer it, and when Mark said, "Oh, there you are, you're home!" she blurted out, "You've got the wrong number, Mark," and hung up. But all right, all right. After that, they called first.

After that morning, she told herself she was going to toughen up – stop thinking about what happened at Susie's funeral, go through with her retirement plans and stop worrying. Surviving what she secretly thought of as her near-death pantry experience gave her courage. If she were making up a greeting card about it, she would have said **"The worst Has Happened — You're Safe!"**

because she had always imagined that when one big thing goes wrong, the mischief gods are satisfied. She was off the radar. Nothing else would happen to her while she had this "worst case scenario" ankle fracture.

And then something did. On September 11, a plane slamming into the North Tower of the World Trade Center interrupted the morning. She was in the kitchen and had turned away from the screen to pour coffee and might have missed it but for the newsreader's frenetic tone. They were already into the drama, exclaiming over how the plane could have miscalculated, flying so low, asking what happened to air traffic control, to cause what they assumed was a catastrophic accident. She switched to CNN and watched as they ran and re-ran the plane crashing into the building, on a seemingly endless loop, as if they couldn't get enough of it; and so fifteen minutes later she watched a second plane crashing into the South Tower thinking it was just rehashing the first. But then it became clear, and everyone knew it was another plane, and this was no accident, and we were under attack. Though was it New York, or America? Was it terrorists or some angry loser? News began to come in that the Pentagon had been attacked. And another plane, headed for the White House, was diverted by passengers and crashed in Pennsylvania. It was unbelievable, awful, exciting. The stuff of movies.

Then the city began to sort itself out. The first responders responded as the city bosses started locking down public venues. They shut the bridges and tunnels and cleared the subways of people. Police were suddenly everywhere. FDNY Rescue One was in Battery Park and other Fire and Police rescue units were in midtown.

When Sally first saw it on the small television in the kitchen, she thought of herself – how good it was she was not downtown or in mid-commute. She was even mildly excited by the breaking news, feeling a little welcome shock in the middle of her ordinary morning, that this was something different from her every day, an excuse to think about something new.

When what had really happened hit her, she watched on the big television in the dark living room, switching from channel to channel, the portable phone in her cold hands, every few minutes trying to reach one of her children: Emily in Queens, Francine at her insurance office in Long Beach, Mark in the city somewhere. Even though she knew none of them were anywhere near the Towers, someone might have been. She called and called.

Everything was moving fast, and at the same time standing still. Sally lost track of how long she sat and watched the reports flow in. There was no way to escape it, no channel that didn't carry it. Like the day John Kennedy was assassinated, everyone was locked into that inescapable black holiday together. Time was canceled by unspoken consent, like a dentist appointment in a blizzard. You couldn't avoid it. In some way, Sally thought, that was a comfort because everyone was in this thing together. When the whole world is crazy, one can actually feel... not sane, exactly, but at least *same.*

She watched the reports of the people who were missing or dead: businessmen, administrative assistants, computer techs, waiters, all unsuspecting, all just going in for a routine day at work. How many tourists were at breakfast at Windows on the World? How many accountants on an elevator to their offices? What were the big stories? Soon enough the media organized itself to tell its stories: visitors looking forward to a patriotic moment at the Ellis Island Museum, maybe taking a selfie, or buying a small flag or T-shirt to commemorate a beautiful day in New York City? Someone on his birthday who didn't have to, coming to the observation deck to see what the city looked like from the top of the world? Children quarantined for hours in their classrooms all over the city, because no one knew whether it was safe for them to go home, and their parents couldn't get them because they were themselves maimed or dead or the bridges and tunnels were closed and no one knew which? The stories were heavy with almosts and if-onlys and but-for-this... thats and other heartbreaking ironies and Sally found herself crying, often, without knowing it until she tasted the salt. There were instant heroes: a ferry boat captain who relayed boatload after boatload of frightened people away from downtown, a subway conductor who managed to lead his passengers away from the Fulton Street Station and out of the tunnel to safety. A man from Tulsa walked away from the conflagration in a daze, devastated, and yet Sally could see that he was slightly thrilled, too, to be right there in the thick, choking on the dust that followed him, not yet aware of the stinging burns on his left arm, eagerly talking to the reporters, smiling shyly into the camera. Behind him was his wife and child, their eyes gritty and wide with shock. *You idiot*, she thought, even though a little while ago she too had been captivated by the unfolding horror.

Hours later, everyone was at Sally's house: neighbors, children, grandchildren. Food materialized. It was like a *shiva* or a wake, and they stayed into the night. Her grandson, Robbie, Mark's son, had been at Stuyvesant High School all day, watching it happen on a TV in the library. One of Mark's childhood friends was a firefighter with Rescue 1; Mark kept trying to reach him. Emily's college roommate had been planning to go to a teachers' rally downtown and Emily kept trying to contact her. It was like touching live wire, but they couldn't help seeking out these connections, they could not leave them alone. It was deplorable but human, Sally thought. So they ate and drank and repeated what they heard, who they knew, and watched the endless loops of terrible stories on television from all over the city. Who would claim ownership of it? Was it leftist or rightist? Foreign or domestic? And over it all was the randomness, and the worry that more was to come, one more renegade plane, one more crazy plot.

When everyone finally left, Sally went upstairs to try and sleep. It suddenly occurred to her that Mr. Foster, the tax preparer who occupied the only other storefront office on her block downtown lived near the Fulton Street Station. Was he there this morning? Was he all right? He had been Sally's neighbor for more than thirty years, though they had only nodded in passing. But recently she heard that his wife had died, and she had been meaning to go in and tell him she was sorry.

"Don't Put Off Until Tomorrow What You Should Do Today."

So, two weeks after it happened, still in a cast and holding onto a cane, Sally took a car service downtown to see her store.

Her children did not know she was doing this. They warned her. The air was bad. There was a heavy police presence at the Federal Reserve, and along Battery Park, and all over the city, as if someone knew something might happen again. They said better safe than sorry (a saying she had taught them) and they wanted her to be safe. They said they *trusted* that they didn't have to tell her not to go because she was smart enough to know better, but saying it told her that they didn't trust her at all. Before all this had happened, she had hired a cleaning service to get her place ready and help her pack up her belongings for her upcoming sale, but now they said it might be months before they got to her, and she did not want to wait. Even though she was hobbled by her injury, there were things to be done. There was all that inventory in flimsy open boxes – thousands of greeting cards filled with words to the wise, righting of wrongs, good advice, her whole life's work – and she didn't want it getting damp and moldy. **"A Wall Is Nothing but a Stack of Bricks**

– Take it One Brick at a Time." A great sentiment for a card, and also true, she thought. If she worked slowly, she could get it done. She would pack all her inventory into plastic crates so the cleaning service could do its work. She took the folded-up crates with her, and told herself this was why she had come. But it was more than that. She wanted to see it for herself.

Downtown was covered with a fine ash made up of pulverized structures, machines, people – like an open-air crematory, she thought. Too quiet. There was her street, her storefront door, the sign SEASONED GREETINGS barely visible in the ash-covered window, even the red car which had been parked illegally in front of the place for a month (and about which she called the D.O.T. several times) still there, though it too, was covered in ash, hardly red anymore at all.

She had inherited the business from her father when it was a small printing shop, designing Christmas cards for the businesses in the area. Little by little she began writing her own greetings, inventing new cards and categories. She had a knack for it, always loved words, loved to play with them and make them rhyme, or capture a feeling, or a thought. People who worked in the neighborhood used to stop in all the time and the things they said, the words they used, found their way into her cards. She knew how to boil down a sentiment so people could know how they felt.

"There Is Nothing Like Physical Work to Remind You That You Aren't Young." She tried emptying file cabinets sitting on a chair, but it made her lightheaded. Once she tried getting down on her good knee and she couldn't get up, and when she grabbed the corner of a table for leverage, she almost pulled it over on top of her. After that, she limited herself to piling files into the boxes and leaving them where they stood. The air in the place was musty and she couldn't stop thinking *what is in this air I'm breathing?* Which was making it hard to take a deep breath. Soon she decided to stop and get some lunch.

In the early days, she had spent lunch hours browsing the department store Montgomery Ward, or the sewing machine repair center, or the small second-hand bookstore next door, with the illegal side entrance and rickety spiral staircase that led to an attic with no heat and piles and piles of as-yet-unsorted books. In 1974, she bought a portable Singer sewing machine for twenty-five bucks. She didn't sew much, but she loved the curvy black machine with the floral design, and the bentwood cover which fitted over it. She still had it.

Sometimes she walked over to Trinity Churchyard and wandered among the graves. People used to eat lunch with the dead in the spring. She had "borrowed" some nifty greeting card sayings from time to time from the headstones. *Dust is dead but spirit lives.* She had been walking around with that one in her head for years. What uncompromising soul had it chiseled in stone above where her husband lay? It was so true, she thought. But who would want to buy a condolence card that said that?

Today, she hobbled around the corner to the sandwich shop she used to order from. She could have picked up the phone, but the truth was, she was as hungry for people to talk to as for something to eat. She wanted someone to whom she could say, "Isn't it terrible?" or "Do you believe it?" or "Unbelievable!" or "Has anyone seen Mr. Foster? The tax preparer?"

One of the countermen said he heard that Mr. Foster might have been killed. "Are you sure?" she said, but he didn't answer, and when she heard someone say, "It was raining people," she left.

Back at her place, she gathered her stuff, locked up and called the car service to take her home. Then, wrapping a scarf around her nose and mouth, with a piece of paper towel she carried out with her she wiped soot off the back of the red car until she could read the license plate; she wrote the numbers down on the back of a store receipt. She didn't know why.

All the way home she thought about the late spring afternoon, the last time she almost – in a long list of almost – went in to say hello to the tax preparer.

"Hello, Mr. Foster," she would have said. "I'm Sally Battel, from SEASONED GREETINGS."

He would have said he knew who she was.

"I just wanted to stop by and tell you how sorry I was to hear that your wife had died," she would have said.

He was a grumpy looking, peculiar looking man. His hair stood straight up from his scalp, in unruly spikes and spokes of different size.

He might have said, "You're a little late. She died a month ago." Or frowned when she said "died" instead of "passed" which people seem to prefer. (The cards she made that said "died" didn't sell but she made them anyway.)

There are people whose presence you get so used to that when they are gone, you miss them even when you barely knew them. She felt the loss of Mr. Foster. *Condolences to me*, she thought.

There should be condolence cards for people who feel loss but have no status. **"Our Heart Goes Out to You on Losing Your Hairdresser of Many Years." "Sorry for the Loss of the Panhandler on Your Corner." "No One Thinks You Are Foolish for Mourning Mr. Foster."**

* * *

She thought, after this new awful turn of events sank in, she would settle down. She would keep her promise to herself, go back to her original plan, recede and retire. She would regain her focus and feel sure about things, about not being depressed. Maybe she would try to find out who belonged to the red car. Or at least why she cared.

Then the dithering of her insides, brain and bowel, would stop. Until then, she just had to hold on. She tried to accept what everyone was saying, that this assault on the city and their lives was the cause of all the depression and upset people were feeling. But she knew there was something else going on. She couldn't name it, but she didn't like it, because when Sally couldn't name something, she could not get a handle on it. Was the craziness of her children's lives getting to her? Their unhappinesses, their divorce threats? But she knew it wasn't that. In the light of the immense upheaval of the explosions, how could it be? Proportionately, it was nothing. She reflected on how a thing could be unchanged but temporarily made smaller by the bigness of something else. If anything, she was worrying less these days about the domestic minutiae of hers or her children's lives.

She concluded it had to be just getting used to living in a world of mornings and afternoons, making up projects, wasting time. She missed the usual noise, and that was why it was so hard to concentrate, or even think without the background music of the city in her ears. She kept the television on, for company. When she turned it off, the quiet in the house was like an over-inflated balloon. She felt an imminent explosion every minute and every minute it didn't come.

* * *

One day Sally went to the mall. She saw a big promotion going on at the Landry Honda at the south end. The windows were papered with "WE'VE GONE APE!" signs and red and yellow banners, and they were giving out free bananas. There was an attractive red car on a turntable. She thought she might take a banana to eat on the way home. She was wearing a new boot over her cast, and felt steady enough, leaning on her cane, but as she got closer, the psychedelic signs and rotating car and buzzing noise of people and neon put her on the edge of vertigo and she felt she had to get away. When she turned to leave, a pigeon-toed gorilla wearing Adidas blocked her way. She tried to go around him, and he came right up to her, so close that she had to put her hand on his chest to make him stop. As Emily might have put it, he was "invading her private space." The costume hair was coarse and greasy. The gorilla leaned against her hand and grunted "Sally."

Sally said, "What?" and the gorilla said her name again. Nasal, and a little phlegmy, like her neighbor Fred. The gorilla cleared his throat. She said, "Fred? What are you doing in there?" and Fred said something that sounded like "beanarillo."

Being a gorilla was the last thing she would have suspected of Fred. He was a retired accountant, for God's sake. A chimp, maybe, but a gorilla? Her real friend had been his wife, Ann, who died last year. Maybe this was one of Fred's seven stages of grief.

He took a break and they went to lunch. Sally let him have it. Ten years her junior and acting senile already! Retired too early! Too much time on his hands! Ought to go back to work, as the kids say, get a life! "A gorilla?" she said. "What were you thinking? What was in that head of yours?"

He shrugged and said it killed time. Filled time. That there was nothing wrong with it.

There were so many things wrong with it she didn't know where to start. "What if you have a heart attack or a stroke and they have to scrape you up looking like this and your poor children have to come and identify you?"

He was eating a Biggy Big Super Sandwich and the special sauce was all over his chin. His pepper and salt hair was flat across his head, and a few coarse pubic-looking gorilla hairs were stuck to his cheek. She took a napkin to brush them off and all of a sudden had to restrain herself from smacking his face. She kept thinking "no wonder" but didn't know what the rest of it was. No wonder people make jokes about older people and retirement? *Filling his time?* Really? She asked him what his children thought about it.

24

"I didn't tell them," he said.

"Aha," she said. "See?"

He asked her not to say anything to them and she agreed. But then, thinking about it later that evening, she gave his daughter, Marcie, a call.

After that, he wouldn't talk to her. When he saw her, he turned his back. If he was waxing his car, or woodworking with the garage door open, one or the other of which he did almost every day, and Sally went over, he dropped what he was doing and by the time she got across the street he was back in the house. She gave it time but he wouldn't budge. She tried phoning but he hung up. Finally, she hobbled over and knocked on the door. Through the window, she saw the lights in the living room; she saw him go into the kitchen. The door was unlocked. She went in. She hadn't been there since Ann died. It looked different. The dust made the furniture look smaller. She smelled cigar smoke. She said, "Fred come out of the kitchen, I'm here to apologize." He came out of the kitchen.

He said, "What do you want?" and she said, "I'm sorry I told Marcie about your gorilla thing. But Ann wouldn't have wanted you to be a gorilla."

"Ann isn't here," he said. "I did what Ann told me for many years and I don't have to do it anymore." That startled her a little.

"Well... I don't want you to do it," she said, though honestly, she didn't give a damn. But she was on a roll... some kind of a roll, and she had to see it through, make her point. "It's below your dignity, Fred."

He looked down like he was measuring the height of his dignity and he said, "Blow yours, Sally, and get the hell out of my house."

She could not believe this was Fred talking. Her ears burned, and her head felt stuffed, there was an echo and her vision slipped for a second, and something on the coffee table broke and when her head cleared, she was standing outside and Fred had closed the door behind her. But after that, the very next day in fact, everything was fine, and the next time Fred was working in his garage, he waved. A few days later Emily, said, "I understand you and Freddy had a real blowout."

"It was just a discussion," she said.

"Not what I heard," Emily said.

"What did you hear?" Sally said.

"Marcie said you threw a dish at him."

"That's ridiculous," Sally said. "It slipped out of my hand." Emily raised her eyebrows.

"You don't believe me?" Sally said.

"Of course I do," Emily said. "Why would you lie?"

"Exactly. Why would I?" Sally said. But for a moment she got confused and thought she had asked herself the question.

* * *

Sally heard from the man who stood next to her at Susie's funeral. He was a pharmacist at Mt. Sinai Hospital and he invited her to a dinner-dance there, and even though she was still in a soft cast, she accepted. He was nice looking, dark haired and neat, and reminded her slightly of Artie, who was also dark-haired and neat. And dapper. As Artie had been, too. And although he was a bit stiff – he brought his CV along in case she wanted to look at it – it was pleasant to sit beside him. They were at a table with people who also seemed familiar to her. They were all of an age, give or take ten years. The women were well put together and the men, too – neat, with the exception of the one across from her, who was artfully shaggy: gray curly hair, a little too long at the neck, and a faded pink V-neck cashmere over an open shirt. No tie. At a dinner-dance. Post-collegiate by about forty years, Sally thought. A familiar type, and familiar himself, she was thinking, it had been nagging at her all evening where she knew him from. Then, right before dessert, it hit her. She realized he was Artie's oncologist, Dr. Joe Messinger. She said his name, and hers, and he did a double take, then got up and came around the table to her. She felt like throwing up. She had not seen him since the day Artie died. Surprised by her sudden emotion, she could hardly speak.

"Dr. Joe," she said, struggling to her feet, leaning on her cane. He grabbed her in a hug, and she almost toppled. "Sally Battel. Pretty as ever," he said.

Composed now, she was glad to see him. "How are you, Dr. Joe?"

He pointed at the cane. "I'm fine," he said. "What happened to you?"

Sally shrugged. "Nothing serious," she said. "Broke my ankle. Fell into an open grave."

He grinned. "Oh, well, that," he said. "Happens all the time. If I had a good gall bladder for every time that happened, I'd be a rich man."

"Exactly," she said. "There you go," and they both laughed. This was the familiar tone he had taken with her all the time he was taking care of Artie, slightly jokey, as if they had agreed to pretend things weren't serious. She had liked teasing him, challenging the exaggerated respect with which people spoke to doctors. She might insult his handwriting, or comment on the pace of his rounds. If he didn't spend enough time, she might raise her eyebrows and say, "What, this is Family Feud and we're playing the lightning round?" And no matter how close to nasty her playfulness got, he never seemed to notice, he was always willing to play along. It had ended up keeping her spirits up, and she had been grateful to him for it. At other times it had hidden how she had hated him, for being so cheerful, handsome, healthy, and unable to do anything to make Artie's cancer go away. That curly-haired doll of a doctor, walking out of the room and leaving them there, finished with the meds, finished with the banter, headed home for the night.

She and Artie used to make fun of him, sometimes. "Dr. Joe College," Artie called him. He probably had a closetful of identical green corduroy jackets with brown suede elbow patches. They used to play "find the stain" because there was always one, on his tie, on his shirt. Of course, they liked him a lot, loved him they often said (the way people say about their doctors, *Oh, we LOVE him, he's like family*, hoping for some extra healing mojo through it) and there was no malice in the game; it had just been a way to lighten the mood.

There was a little spot of lobster bisque on his sweater, and she smiled, thinking how Artie would have enjoyed the moment.

"Ah, those pretty dimples," Dr. Joe said, patting her hand. And then he was taking off abruptly, after a slim, blondish woman heading toward the door, waving hastily, saying he had to go, saying how great it was to see her. She tried to get a look at the wife, but couldn't see much more than the back of her: slim and chic. Doctor's wife basic. The encounter was nice, and funny, but left her shaken, with a feeling she couldn't write a greeting card for, because she wouldn't know what words to use.

* * *

Sally went to rehab for her foot. She went into it thinking she wouldn't like it, but she did. She loved it. She loved the bright, airy room with hanging plants in front of the big windows, and the way the therapist moved around from one person to another, like he was choreographed. It was a big sunny place, like a studio, or a gym, but a nice, kind, gentle gym with no young perfect bodies, and no overachievers, just a whole bunch of mostly over-age, post-surgical injurees and chronic complainers. She loved the woman who had carpal tunnel surgery, who worked her finger a quarter of an inch and grunted like she was moving a piano. She loved the guy who was coming off a back injury and every time he did a squat he passed wind, and every time he passed wind he cleared his throat as if that would hide the sound. She loved the man who whistled through his teeth from the minute he lumbered up the stairs, through his treadmill routine, and all the way through putting his jacket back on, stopping at the desk to make another appointment, whistle, whistle, whistle. She loved the big blue stretchy rubber bands that she had to rest her foot in and pull and do re-habby tricks with. When the therapist complimented her on her range of motion in the healing ankle, it made her day. "Remarkable," he said. It was maybe the first time anyone used that word to describe anything about her, ever. She felt so much affection for one and all the rehabbers that she could not refrain from calling out encouragement. Nothing big deal, just "that's better than last week," and "looking good," things like that. Which, as it turned out, she wasn't supposed to do. The therapist took her aside. He said there had been complaints and one person had even changed his day because of her. (She noticed the whistler was gone and had worried.) The therapist said there was an unspoken zone of privacy even though they were all in the same room.

* * *

"In other words, I'm supposed to pretend I don't hear the man with the back issues fart every time he does a squat?"

Emily sighed. Sally made the mistake of telling her what the therapist said and of course Emily was siding with the therapist. "Yes, Mom. It's called privacy. And I'm sure they don't appreciate you watching their every move, either," Emily said.

"It's a survivor's room," Sally explained. "We've all fallen and we've all gotten up, see? And it's not like a gym, where everyone's firm and fit. We're all swollen and stiff. It tickles me, that's all. I'm just being friendly, Emmy," she said.

"That's what worries me," Emily said. "It's not like you to be so democratic."

* * *

At dinner with Bradley, the pharmacist, looking for something to talk about, she told him the story, making it amusing. "My daughter said it isn't like me to do that," she said. He smiled, but she could see he sided with Emily, too. He said wasn't she fortunate to have such a concerned daughter, worrying about her mother's inappropriate behavior. She clarified that Emily meant it wasn't like Sally to be so indiscriminately friendly. "I'm usually a little more buttoned up," she explained.

"What our children think they know about us... and don't," he said, and straightened his tie. "But it demonstrates how much regard your daughter has for you, for her to evince such concern."

"What it demonstrates," Sally said, laughing, "is how she meddles in my life." Later, she said it wasn't necessary for him to show her to her door, but he insisted. And when he drew close, she let him kiss her. Afterward she thought it was fine. It wasn't sex, and it wasn't affection; but it was fine anyway, like a handshake with lips.

The interview... Her favorite grandchild, CJ – Caroline Jane – called from college. She is doing a psychology project and wanted to ask some questions.

Sally was happy to oblige. "What do you want to know?"

"Are you happy?"

Sally did not answer at once. Not that she didn't know, just that she didn't want to say the wrong thing to this impressionable child whom she loved. But finally: "I don't think so. No."

"Why not?"

"I'm not unhappy," she said. "I'm content. I'm grateful for all the good things I've had in life – Grandpa Artie, my kids, you grandkids, my business, some friends, good skin, good genes... all the cliches. But happy? No."

CJ's voice was muffled, and Sally pictured her taking notes and holding the phone in the crook of her neck. "Next, what do you crave, what gives you pleasure?"

"Well, I don't know that I crave anything... I don't remember ever really craving things, even when I was young. Well, that's not really accurate. I think what I crave is contentment." Even as a girl, Sally was drawn to small things, mild pleasures. The pencil groove in her grade school desk, she recalls sliding her finger along it, thinking this is nice. "A precocious dullness," she said, with a little laugh. (And as she told her granddaughter this, she had a sudden thought she was lying. No, not lying, forgetting something, or fudging it.) But she went on. "I often thought my biggest desire was to be the opposite of your great-grandmother, who was glamorous. Always with the drama. Does that sound silly?"

"No, Gran. That's just the way I feel."

"Hmm. I wouldn't have thought so," Sally said. Not this child who always seemed to be in the center of a storm, often of her own making. "What's this questionnaire about anyway?"

"It's family tendencies. We're supposed to make one statement about ourselves and then examine it in the light of three relatives we closely identify with."

"I'm flattered you asked me, honey. Who else?"

She had chosen her brother, Robbie, and her Aunt Fran.

"What about your dad?" Sally didn't like to think of her son being left out.

"Oh, Dad's too easy," CJ said. "I'm like his clone."

Sally hoped she wasn't, but didn't say so. "Well, good. I thought it might be you were mad at him."

CJ laughed again. "Not this week," she said.

31

It was good to hear her sounding cheerful. She had a rotten first year at school and there had been some concern. Away from home, away from New York. None of her high school friends went to Pitt and she had struggled with loneliness. She even had a short bout of not eating, which Sally's daughter-in-law had been too quick (and with a little too much satisfaction) to label anorexia. Always with the labels, some people. But there you go, anorexia doesn't come and go like the flu, does it? And time had taken care of whatever was wrong. "You sound good, honey," Sally said. "Not so... turbulent. If that's the right word. What is your statement that you are examining? Can I ask?"

CJ was silent and Sally could hear her breathing and shuffling papers. Outside the window, the sharp autumn sun switched itself off, abruptly, and the afternoon turned slate. And then a cardinal flew by. Ahhhh, perfect! Sally thought, smiling.

"I don't have to be happy to be happy," CJ said. The statement had a bright, aphoristic quality, but Sally was not sure what it meant. You have to be very specific for the statement to work.

"Are you saying you can be happy as long as you're not miserable?"

"No. I mean I was not put on this earth to be happy. It isn't an end that I recognize."

"What were you put on this earth for?" The brass letter opener made a perfect leg scratcher. It would have slid all the way down her calf inside the cast. Why hadn't she thought about it when she needed it?

"To be productive," CJ answered without hesitation.

"Just what Grandpa Artie would have said," Sally said. "But isn't that just tailoring the meaning of 'happiness' to fit yourself? Aren't you saying you have to be productive to be happy?"

There seems to be trouble on the line. CJ's voice sounds tinny and far away.

"What do you think you were put on this earth for, Granny?"

she said.

The cardinal is gone, and the sun returns in a wave of light, and then suddenly it seemed like a story which was either going to end with the cardinal's return or the maintenance of sun. Hope is the thing with feathers Sally thought. There must be a thousand greeting cards that used that quote.

"Gran?"

"I don't think I was put on this earth for anything at all. I think you make up the 'for' as you go along. Nothing preordained. Everything just is."

"That sounds very fatalistic," CJ said. "Do you still miss Grandpa Artie?"

Sally does, some days, and some days he was emphatically there with her, and she didn't have to miss him, as when she cooked. (Which she didn't do much anymore.) And some days she was glad to be rid of him, as any wife, even a loving one is glad to be rid of a husband on say, an ordinary Wednesday, when she had things to do and thoughts to think. Artie had been high maintenance in some ways. "Some days," she said.

"Did you ever feel you didn't want to go on without him?"

"Oh, my. No. Never."

And then CJ had to go, and Sally was left with an open cupboard full of thoughts.

* * *

The red car really played on Sally's mind What if there had been a baby in the back of the car? Had she ever looked in the windows to see? Had the owner died sometime before 9/11? Was he blameless because he was dead?

The specter of divorce loomed on the horizon... All three of Sally's children were heading for divorce. And what was that about?

Sally considered the inadvisability of retiring... She

never should have done it. Sixty-eight was too young. It was disorienting to think she was retired, to say it, to be it. She was beginning to feel old. She thought about death. She worried about every last detail of her health, got beside herself if she got a little headache, or stomach ache, or stepped wrong, or forgot a word.

Losing words is a natural thing, however, she was far from aphasic. Of all the people she knows, she was the most wordly. (A play on worldly, not a mistake.) Hell, she could give up half her vocabulary and still have more words than most people. But now that she had retired her greeting card company, there was no place to play with words, to use them. So from time to time, a word dropped out, for a minute, or an hour, or a day, which was nothing to worry about. Her former assistant, Ginny, who died when she was eighty-eight and had all her marbles and worked right up to the end, had been losing words for years. She substituted the word "thing" for what she couldn't remember, and after a couple of scotches it got worse. So it would sound like, "When I was thing, I used to clock in and go down thing, get my hair done, and come back and no one in the office knew. I had thing." When she was in the hospital, dying, she said to Sally, "Pull the thing," and Sally didn't know whether she meant the call bell or the plug. The other day Sally wasted hours trying to come up with the last name of Mandy who played thing in thing. Patinkin. Che Guevara. Evita.

Dead tired, she reviewed and reviewed and reviewed as the clock ticked on. Over the years she had written so many great cards, so many sayings. They were pieces of advice, really. Ways to solve the problems of life. You said them like you were waving a wand – the saying tells you what to do. So why wasn't it working now?

Selling the company had been a mistake, she saw that now. Not only because it meant retirement, but because it meant the end of doing something she loved. It upset her more than widowhood. She had built it from a single card into a well-known niche company. Everyone in the business knew her. This, in the days when women didn't build businesses so much as they do now. And her cards were good. She was the first one to make cards for same sex marriage, mothers' and fathers' day cards appropriate for multiple mothers and fathers, and her grouping of "Heard you were out..." with illustrations of barred windows (nuthouse or jailhouse or zoo or closet), was a good seller. Now, if she wanted appreciation for all she had done and who she was, she was going to have to boast about it, and that, Sally told herself, she would never do.

National Greetings promised to keep her line of cards intact, but they lied. The first thing they did was discontinue the nuthouse grouping; her same sex cards were down to a single one. She can't sue, as has been suggested to her. She based the agreement on a handshake and there was nothing in the paperwork that would hold them to it. She felt like a fool.

Too Tired to Cook... skips in her thoughts where the print dropped out and she couldn't read the whole of what she was thinking. When it happened it was inconvenient and resulted in mistakes. Today, preparing dinner for the family, for example. She was as usual, doing three things at once, and suddenly she forgot how to assemble the food mill for a few seconds. Of course it came right back, the memory reassembling itself like a word that now and then seems strange and then doesn't. Then she put the food mill together as always. But it left her with a dry mouth. What is that phrase, you're in front of the audience and they aren't laughing? Flop sweat? She wiped her brow and milled the cooked carrots. Don't worry, don't worry. After all, she had not used the food mill in more than a year. She was making this special dinner for Rita, her sister-in-law, her late brother's wife, who was seventy-eight and had survived a bout of breast cancer and was now not feeling well. "I'd better do it now," she said, "because what if I wait until I feel like it, and Rita dies before that day comes?" To atone for her impure thoughts, she was going all out. Julia Child's vegetarian gateau, very labor intensive, a boned, rolled leg of lamb, even homemade bread. Her famous Linzer tarts. And all the time thinking how many dinners have I cooked in my lifetime? How many have I wanted to cook? How many have I done like this, as an atonement or an obligation or an apology or a plea?

"I'm not cooking anymore," she announced, surprising herself.

Her son, Mark, laughed.

"What's so funny, Mark?" she said.

"Do you know how many times you've said that?" he said.

She doesn't. She remembers no times. But she said, "Well this time is different. This time I mean it. I'm tired of cooking."

"You've said that, too," he said.

Relentless, the memory of one's children. She will have to remember to remember to remember not to tell them so much, she thought. "Next time I won't say it, I'll just do it," she said.

"You've said that, too," Mark said, but she did not know if it was true or he was just being... something.

He came early. To tell her something, she felt. She could always feel when Mark had something special to say. He *attended* to her. She was impatient to find out why, this time, but she did not ask. She left him in the living room with a drink, while she went upstairs to dress. She once dyed her hair. At times she has been brunette, blonde, streaked blonde, auburn, but now she had turned that lucky shade of pure white and leaves it alone. It was cropped short and CJ taught her how to put some gel in it so it looked spiky and up-to-date. ("Otherwise you're just another tennis grandma," CJ said.) Her face was not smooth, but not too lined; tired-pretty she thought, looking in the mirror. Her mother always said men prefer a pretty face to a shapely body. A woman can lie and still project the truth with blue eyes or a dimpled smile. She smoothed some makeup on, one of a handful of jars she bought from time to time and rarely used, to make herself look less tired. She changed out of her jeans into a silk shirt and a pair of trousers. She has invited the pharmacist and she wanted to look nice, though she was not sure she liked him enough for that to make any sense. She was slightly off balance. Usually when this happened, she asked whatever one of her children was around to assess whether she was walking cockeyed. But she didn't want to ask Mark. She was still technically confined to sturdy shoes, like sneakers, but she said what the hell and slipped on a pair of old flats: not exactly glamorous, like the shoes lady trainers wear to walk their poochies around the Westminster Dog Show. But better than sneakers. She was still limping. She ran her hand through her hair and slowly brushed mascara on her lashes. By the time she came downstairs, the rest of the company was there, and she was safe from Mark's confidences and her own concern. Aside from Rita and her boyfriend, Bob, and Mark, there was Fran (her husband, Dan, couldn't make it) and Emily and Fred. Bradley called to say he was running late. "Due to an unexpected conflict," he said.

Fred looked different. She couldn't figure out what it was at first, but then she realized it was a new kind of haircut, like a marine. A buzz cut. Attractive. "You have a nice head, Fred," she said, trying not to sound surprised.

Not that it made him any less boring. She kept trying to draw him into the conversation. In desperation, she asked him what kind of Simonize he uses on his car to get it so shiny and that seemed to lower some conversational drawbridge and he crossed over with a most bizarre account of a fight he almost had at the local car wash when he asked for a Deluxe wax and polish and they left streaks all over his hood.

In the midst of it Sally pretended she forgot something in the kitchen so she could get away from the monotony of his voice. When she came back, everyone was in stitches, Emily whooping and snorting, her cheeks rosy. "What'd I miss?" Sally said, but everyone was too busy laughing to pay any attention.

Then the doorbell rang. It was the pharmacist, Bradley, with an armful of bottles of red wine and a bulldog on a leash.

"I'm deeply apologetic," he said, "but I could not find a sitter for Fletcher. My kennel has banned him. And I didn't know what else to do. I really wanted to attend."

"Why has your kennel banned him? Oh, never mind, Bradley, come in, both of you. We're glad you decided to come. We're just starting dinner. Let me put down some water for the dog."

"I brought my own bowl," Bradley said.

Bradley had a very precise way of talking. At first, Sally thought it was ironic, using big words when small ones would do, or saying dates and times like he was footnoting his life. "On Tuesday, April 3, 2013, I underwent a colonoscopy performed by Dr. Samuel Tisch." As if saying, "Could I ever forget such a thing?" ironically. But she was beginning to realize that he was quite literal and dead serious. "By previous arrangement, I delivered my French bulldog, Fletcher, to Main Street Veterinarians, signing in at exactly ten-oh-three," he said. "I proceeded to wait until eleven-forty-three, fully one hour and forty minutes later. At which time I approached the window and inquired as to when Fletcher would be admitted, for his stay. He was to undergo a sleep study and would be accommodated overnight."

"What'd he do, pee on the floor?" Fran said, impatient to cut to the chase.

"Fee-seed," Bradley corrected.

Rita was hard of hearing but refused to ask people to repeat themselves. She said, "How nice."

Bradley, who was crosshatching his mashed potatoes with his fork, and, who Sally guessed was somewhat hard of hearing himself, said, "Thank you."

"What part of France is the dog from?" Rita asked.

Dessert was a disaster. The Linzer tarts, her specialty, were awful. "They don't taste sweet," Rita said. "Did you cut back on the sugar?"

Sally said she did, but she knew immediately what had happened. She forgot to add any sugar at all.

"Well, you can't fritz around with recipes," Rita said. "It's better to eat half of the original thing than try and eat a lousy dietetic version. Not that these are lousy, Sal," she said.

Sally laughed. "But they are," she said, taking the platter of them off the table before anyone else could eat one. "I think I have some Chips Ahoy in the pantry. Too bad I don't have any ice cream. We could make sandwiches."

Fred said he had some Haagen-Dazs in his freezer. "Don't get up, I'll go across and get it," Emily said.

"Emmy, I'm not an old man," Fred said. "I can go."

"Well, I want some fresh air, so I'll go with you," she said.

Sally thought Emily might be smoking again; she thought she smelled tobacco on her when she came in.

* * *

Desperate for sleep, Sally took one of Artie's leftover pills. The kind people say can sometimes make you sleepwalk or sleep-eat or sleep-drive or sleep-cook. She broke it in half and took the smaller half. And she slept. In the morning, she found she had taken her underpants off. They were on the floor beside the bed.

* * *

Dead tired, again she reviewed and reviewed and reviewed, and finally took another half pill. She dreamt of having an orgasm. She feels the electricity and release in her sleep, and she woke so rested and relaxed, it was as good as a real one. And her underpants were off again, on the floor beside her bed.

It made her laugh to think that though the pill didn't make her sleepwalk or -eat or -cook, she was multitasking, anyway.

* * *

So all three of her children were getting divorced.

"Is this my fault?" Sally asked Emily.

"Why does everything have to be about you?" Emily said, rather more testily than usual.

"Because it is about me, in a way. Who raised you? Who taught you? Who gave you your values? And why are you being so snappy? You sound like Francine." Emily is usually gentle, Fran is more... bottom line. Emily is Sally's, Fran belongs to Artie?

"Sorry, Mom. You and Daddy had a wonderful marriage. You set a perfect example. You were fantastic role models. Is that what you want to hear?"

"Not what I want or don't want, Emmy. What's the truth? And anyway, how do you know what our marriage was like? Maybe it was rotting from within."

That stopped her. "Was it?" she said, at last.

"What? No, it was great," Sally said.

"So maybe we all saw what you and Daddy had and fell short of it and couldn't live with that."

"You think that's what I want to hear? Emmy, stop. If it's not about me it's not about me. Don't make me take the blame just because I want to."

Emily's laugh sounds like a snort, and was the only thing about her which reminded Sally of the child she once was. "But why do you?"

"I guess I just want a reason, or an explanation. It seems so... random... and senseless otherwise."

She looked at her youngest child, once a bringer of light, a barn swallow, swooping and flitting from here to there, filled with happiness. Now she was sitting upright, at the edge of the kitchen chair, swirling the teabag in the last of the tea, making Sally think of drowning things. Her posture, once a dancer's, was now simply stiff. This child of hers, floundering. Too many gifts, Sally thought? How do you help someone with too many gifts? She passed the bar but decided to become a psychologist, and from the looks of it, that didn't make her happy, either. There was nothing Sally could do.

"I guess Keith and I just grew apart, "Emily said, looking at Sally as if to say, *Will that satisfy you? Is that enough?*

"Well," Sally said, standing up, brushing her hands free of the crumbs of troubling thoughts, "I'm not going to fuss about it. You're all adults. I'm just glad one doesn't have to 'attend' a divorce as one does a wedding. I'd have to get three new dresses."

"Very funny," Emily said, not laughing, but clearly relieved the conversation was over.

* * *

Sally took Rita to the doctor. She was recruited – though strictly speaking, she volunteered. Rita had that talent. Sally called it "the Tom Sawyer thing." She could appear so helpless you couldn't help wanting to paint the fence for her.

As she settled herself in the car, she said, "You don't mind going to Mt. Sinai, do you? I mean does it give you flakebacks?"

"Flashbacks?" Sally said. "Now you're asking me? What would you do if I said yes?"

Rita didn't speak. She covered her mouth and slowly shook her head. "I didn't think," she said.

Of course she had thought. But Sally didn't want to turn it into a fight. "That's okay, Ree," she said. "I don't get flashbacks and I don't mind taking you at all. We'll have lunch at Sara's Kitchen after."

"I apologize. I should have said something before," Rita said. "But anyway, let's skip Sara's Kitchen. The last time I was there I think I got food poisoning."

The lobby of the hospital was crowded with people coming and going, and what looked like a new crop of interns in tight formation near the elevators. Rita was brisk. This was her town today. "Follow me," she said and they bypassed the main lobby and followed arrows down long corridors until they came to a suite of offices. The Cancer Group, the sign said. Rita gave a little shiver. "I don't know why they name it that," she said.

It is the same group Artie had gone to, though Rita's doctor is not the same one. The office had been re-located here since Sally's time. Its decor reflected the times. There was an article about it in the current issue of "AARP Today." "Less Like a Hospital, more like a Home" had been the title. Floral pillows on leather couches, billowy curtains instead of blinds. Big deal. As if that could make a difference.

Sally had brought the latest Donna Leone with her, and she made herself comfortable while Rita fussed and played games on her smart phone until her name was called. It was a six-month check-up and she said she had been doing well, though Sally didn't think so, quite. It was about noon, and all but one of the women behind the desk had gone to lunch, and the office was empty, save for her. There was a low buzz of music in the background, mellow, and a slice of sunshine on the arm of the sofa. She put her book aside and closed her eyes. She dozed off and was startled awake by the touch of a hand on her wrist.

"Taking your pulse. Nice and steady." It was Dr. Messinger.

"Hey, Dr. Joe," she said, shaking his hand.

"No more cane?" he said.

"Oh, no, I'm fine now," she said. "I'm actually allowed to wear regular shoes again. Woohoo."

He smiled. Then frowned. "You're not... you aren't here to see me, are you?"

"No, no," she said. "My sister-in-law... Artie's sister is in with Ferguson."

"Oh, okay," he said, and sighed, as if relieved that she hadn't come here with her own cancer. "Do you have time for a coffee?"

She looked at her watch, but just then Rita emerged.

Rita was flushed. "Thumbs up," she said, smiling hard at Sally, including Dr. Joe in her smile. But Sally could see something was not right. Dr. Joe put his hand on Sally's arm like he had seen it, too. "Sorry," he said, "Maybe another time," and nodding at them both, he left them.

Rita was breathing hard, but not ready to talk, Sally could see. "He always had such a nice manner," she said, distractedly, tilting her head toward where he went. "Let's go home, Sal, I'm tired."

Sally helped Rita on with her coat, thinking, oh God, what now?

* * *

CJ called. Sally and her granddaughter had settled into a comfortable rhythm of long talks by phone. "I love that you don't text me," Sally said. "You're an old-fashioned girl."

"I wouldn't hear your voice if I texted," CJ said. "Part of what you say is your wicked delivery, Granny."

"Wicked?" "Me?" Sally said. But she loved it.

"What's up? How's your psych report going?"

"Well, aside from the fact that I can't get Aunt Fran to call me back, it's going fine so far. Robbie came down last weekend and we hung out and talked a lot and I got some great insights."

"In other words, you got your underage brother drunk?" Sally said.

CJ laughed. "Can I read you what I wrote about you?"

"Sure," Sally said.

CJ cleared her throat. *Has anything wonderful happened? That's what my grandmother always said to us kids. It made us try to think of something wonderful to tell her. I realize now she was probably trying to stop us from being negative. Or from telling her something terrible she didn't want to hear.*

There was an anxious silence. "Wow," Sally said. "I didn't know I did it that often. But you're right, I said it to make you kids think positively, and I guess I didn't want to hear anything bad, either. Is there more?"

She could hear CJ hesitate. Then: *My grandma has a smile that's not really a smile. It's a way of holding her mouth that looks like she's smiling, and she has rosy cheeks and her eyes crinkle up at the corner, so people think she is sweet, and she can say anything she wants, be completely honest even if it is negative and people just don't seem to mind.*

Sally, who was lying in bed, tried to see herself in the mirror over the dresser, but even squinting, she was a blur. A smiling blur, she was sure. She laughed. "Oh, I don't really do that, do I?"

"Are you kidding, Gran? I see the way you work my dad."

"Oh, well, he's my kid, CJ. Anyway, I don't mind the description, even if I'm not sure I'm worthy. So what's the family trait?"

"The trait I supposedly inherited from you is honesty, but with my face it isn't so easy. People hate me when I speak up. I'm not beautiful like you."

Dear child. She was so beautiful, but so beaten down by her parents' expectations, she had no idea. She covered herself up in drab, baggy clothes and thought integrity meant not wearing lipstick. And she was so nervous, she pulled on her hair.

"Oh, darling. Thank you. But you *are* beautiful. You can't think you're not. I won't let you."

"Thanks, Granny. I'm not putting myself down, I'm just being honest."

"You're doing both. But what does what I look like have to

do with honesty?"

"Well, you look like you like everyone all the time, so they don't mind you being honest. My face always looks mad."

"In my day, a girl's resting face always had to be smiling. Nowadays, a girl can do anything she wants with her face."

"I never thought of it that way," CJ said. "But I think that's part of what I have a problem with. *Your* day. *My* day. It's bad enough I'm born with my mother's brains and my father's nature instead of the other way around. How am I supposed to grow into my own person if I'm always bound by what came before and what the current line is?"

"I wish there was a way to escape it," Sally said. It occurred to her that once, long ago, she had felt the same way. *Bound,* her granddaughter said. Tied up. Or, what is it she had once called it? *Caught.* How could she have forgotten?

But, it turned out, that is not why CJ has called. She took a deep nervous breath. "Let's have it," Sally said.

"Well, someone I know... is doing an article on 9/11 and maybe it's going to be published and I might have said some things I maybe shouldn't have."

"Like what?" Sally said, thinking *three maybes make a for-sure.*

"I might have mentioned you, and your old office, and how you almost went to work that day... and how devastated you were..."

"You might have? Sounds like you did, CJ."

"I know, Gran. I'm sorry. I should have checked with you to see if it's okay. It's not my story to tell."

"No, it's not, honey. And where did you get the idea that I was devastated, or was that just your take on it?"

"Well, weren't you? Devastated? I thought you were. I thought you still are."

And Sally got a little dizzy, and wondered if she was, if she wasn't, what devastated felt like. Everyone was always saying *devastated this* and *incredible that* and everything lately was a

45

holocaust. Someone in her beauty parlor said the rain over the weekend flooded her basement and it was like a holocaust hit.

"Not the point. You don't know what's in someone else's mind, not even if you are very close. Everyone *is* an island, despite the saying. Everyone is a closed box."

"I'm sorry," CJ said, sounding miserable.

"On the other hand, it's not such a big deal. All is forgiven. Now go to class."

And as they exchange the usual "love yous" and hung up, Sally thought *am I smiling now?*

* * *

Dr. Messinger called to see how Rita was.

"Did you speak to Ferguson?" Sally asked.

He hesitated. He probably did, but he wouldn't admit it. "Do you want me to?" he said.

"No, no, that's all right," Sally said. "It's not my business. I'm not going to pry. It won't make her better."

He let out a breath and sounded relieved. "And now to the main reason I called," he said. "Would you have lunch with me?"

It took her completely by surprise and she said, "Really? Dr. Joe? Why?" Before she could think of how it sounded. Maybe he was forming a support group. She was not interested.

"Why not?" he said.

"I'm sorry," she said. " I didn't mean to be offensive, I just..."

"Wondered why," he said. "I understand. I don't have an agenda, I just thought it would be nice to get together. We have a lot in common."

We do?

"Aren't you married?" Sally said.

"My wife died some time ago," he said.

"I'm sorry," she said.

46

"Well, now that we've gone through the third degree, will you?"

"Will I what?"

"Have lunch. It's just lunch, Sally."

And at that point, she didn't really see how she could say no without being really rude, and no one wants to insult a good oncologist.

"I'd love to, Dr. Joe," she said. Thinking *I'd hate to*.

* * *

"Well, I'm not surprised," Francine said. "He used to flirt with you all the time, in Daddy's hospital room."

"You're nuts," Sally said, but it made her lightheaded to hear Francine say it.

* * *

He picked her up at home. He was wearing jeans and cowboy boots and she thought *welcome to the rodeo* but then felt mean when he greeted her warmly, with a big smile and a hug. He said it was a beautiful day, and proposed a ride out to the beach. She had been lightheaded all morning, and tried to get him to settle for coffee. "I just baked," she said, to tempt him.

"Your chocolate chip cookies?"

She remembered, at the bedside, while Artie had struggled to breathe, she had held the tin with butter-stained napkins, he had dipped his hand in.

"No, come on, come out," he said, and tugged her hand, like a kid, and she couldn't help laughing. "But not all the way to the beach," she said. "There's a nice diner." But the parking lot of the diner was crowded, and when they peered through the window it looked packed.

"We'll never get served," he said. "Come on."

It had been years since she was at Jones Beach in the winter. She and Artie had gone from time to time. Artie would sit on the boardwalk and watch her walk down to the shore in the damp, cold sand, picking her way through glass and broken shells, picking up pretty stones and bits of beach glass as she went. She had gotten the whole collection of them together recently, while she was still stuck in the house, and put them in a glass bowl.

The concession was open and he bought two cups of chowder and a ham sandwich to share, and they sat on a bench facing the sun.

Mostly, Joe talked. He was a widower six years. So, he had been newly widowed when he was taking care of Artie. She wondered how that had felt. He has one child, a son, an internist at Albany Med. She liked the sound of his voice, which was deep and soft, with a strong Brooklyn accent.

Bikers and roller bladers rode back and forth, blocking their sun and every once in a while, he raised his arm as if he were a flagman and waved them on with a smile. He said he missed biking since his knee replacement. Repetitive movement is bad for the knees. Her lightheadedness was gone, and she was relaxed. He asked about Bradley, if she was still seeing Bradley. She was. He said he is a nice man and she said he is a nice man, and then, because she couldn't resist a good story, she told him about the CV, how Bradley had shown up on their first date with a copy of his CV in his tuxedo pocket.

Dr. Joe threw back his head and laughed. "You mean that night? At the dinner dance?"

Sally nodded. "Oh, look, he's a nice man, he's just a little.... precise..." she said.

He laughed again, and said poor Bradley. It was nice, sitting there feeling the sun, watching the water, not feeling the need to speak. But it was clear he had something on his mind.

"I was your late husband's... I was Arthur's doctor," he said. "And I am sorry I could not do better for him."

She had not expected this. Was he apologizing? Because Artie died? What a thing to apologize for. Artie had been in a lot of pain, very weak. Two weeks after the last surgery, they all knew things were not going well, but Dr. Joe had kept on about another protocol and a new trial and further options, and it had been Artie who said to her with exasperation and disbelief, "This guy doesn't give it a rest." Is that what this was all about? Could he not forgive himself because Artie died? Did he think less of Artie because he died after all the doctor's efforts?

Suddenly the whole thing made her blazingly angry, and in that odd misdirection that happens with women, it leaked out her eyes. He leaned over and brushed a tear off her cheek. She smelled aftershave and a slight salinity which might have been sweat or the sea air. "Is that what this is all about?" she said.

"Oh, no, no, no," he said. "I'm doing this very badly. I'm presenting my CV, like Bradley. That's what this is all about."

"Oh, dear, no," she said. "We know each other, don't we?" And now she felt as though she were pleading for the relationship to stay as it was. He was her late husband, Arthur's, ex-doctor. Period. "You don't have to present yourself to me."

"I think I do," he said. "I want to. I was Arthur's doctor, but now I would like to be someone different. I would like to be friends. To... take you out," he said.

They both stared at the ocean, waiting for her tears to dry and the moment of surprise to blow over.

She meant to say that this was not possible. It was not something she had even thought about. It was something she would have to think about. "I think I'd like a drink," she said.

"Scotch?" he said.

"Bourbon," she said. "But yes."

Sally has lived in Bellerose forever. She and Artie had bought the house the year Fran, their oldest child, was born, moving from a spacious apartment in Bayside to this small house, little more than a bungalow. The two of them had grown up in apartments, and dreamed of owning their own home. To Artie, it meant being allowed to bang nails in the wall any time he wanted. (Though once the walls were his, he didn't want to put holes where he might not want them ten or twenty years later, if and when they rehung their pictures.) To Sally, it was all about the backyard, about being able to step outside without going down in an elevator, and not having to smell someone else's pot roast cooking in the hallway.

They had always planned for this to be their "starter" home, but they never moved on. The neighbors became friends, and the schools were good, the commute, at least for Artie, to his midtown office, was easy, so they never could think of a good reason to move. "Uproot" is the word they used, when occasionally the opportunity or the temptation of a bigger house in a richer suburb presented itself. That was in the years when housing developments, like theirs, or most famously like Levittown, were looked down on for their sameness. Sally remembers a folk song about "Little Houses Made of Ticky-Tacky" that Pete Seeger used to sing. But over the years, people made changes to the houses, or their yards, so you could no longer, as the old joke went, stagger home late at night and not know which front door was yours. Fenced yards, hedged yards, flagstone walks, porch rails around the carport, enclosing the carport into a proper garage, added-on rooms, second stories. Yet the neighborhood retained its character, which was neat, middle class, white with tasteful touches of brown, and only one eyesore, where a neighbor had razed a bungalow and put up a McMansion. (Which had been on and off the market for two years now, the price reduced three times.) The trees matured, the median age advanced, but it was still the place Sally had loved since the first time she saw it. She stopped talking like a realtor. "So you don't think it's a little tacky?" she said.

"Are you kidding? I grew up in a house like this. It's what I miss about living in an apartment," Joe said, as he stretched out on the beach chair. They had driven back to Bellerose from Jones Beach, stopping at the corner liquor store for Scotch for him and now they sat, drinking and eating Cheetos in her backyard. It was chilly and the sun was almost gone, but she brought out two afghans and they stayed put. He was even easier to talk to after two bourbons.

"I thought you were apologizing for Arthur's death," she said.

He shook his head. "I wasn't apologizing," he said. "I said I was sorry. That's not the same thing."

"Okay," she said, because she was suddenly too tired to talk.

He stayed a long time, until the buzz wore off, because he didn't want to drive under the influence. She ordered Chinese food and had an abrupt memory of bringing containers of it to the hospital on one of Artie's good days; Dr. Joe had come in licking his chops, following the smell, and they had all agreed that the smell was usually better than the taste. And Artie's appetite had gone away somewhere between the phone call when he said he was hungry and her walking into the room with her arms full. So, Artie had dozed, and she and Dr. Joe had picked at the food. As they did tonight. After he left, she thought how pleasant it was, having him there, talking with him, schmoozing. She hadn't schmoozed in a while. He could be her brother. It was possible. Maybe they could be friends.

* * *

When she couldn't sleep, her mind went from "raining people" to the red car and then to Artie – their life, his death, his dying, mostly, to those days in and out of the hospital when Dr. Joe had been in and out, kind, encouraging, handsome, ready with a joke, terribly, terribly alive.

"Where's your boyfriend tonight?" Artie had whispered to her, jarred awake by some pain or terror.

"My *who*?"

"You know, Joe College," he said.

"Do you want me to call him," she had said, suddenly panicked. "Are you in pain?"

"No, no, no," Artie said, drowsily. "I was just wondering," and he fell back to sleep.

* * *

"I always wondered," Emily said. "Whether Dr. Joe 'helped' Daddy die."

"Oh, I don't think so," Sally said. But she wondered, too.

* * *

Sally asked Fran what happened to her marriage. "Emily said Dad and I had such a perfect marriage that the rest of you can't live up to it," she said.

Fran shook her head. "I always thought you and Dad were mad at each other half the time," she said.

"Oh, dear, no." Sally said. But felt her stomach tighten. "Really?"

Surely Fran was projecting. Fran, her angry child. Fran, the child who never cried, who kept a poker face at all times no matter what.

Succinctly, she answered Sally's question. Dan, her husband, her childhood sweetheart, her best friend and business partner, sabotaged a business deal.

Like a fool, Sally said, "At least he didn't cheat with a woman." She heard it as she said it and tried to stop the words but it was too late. And Fran, the child who never cried, fell apart. She howled. She wouldn't let Sally take her in her arms. She wouldn't take a tissue. She wiped the snot off her face with her arm and kept on crying.

After a while, she stopped, and Sally said, "Tell me what happened."

"But don't criticize," Fran said.

"I won't," Sally said. "Tell me."

Fran took a deep breath and sat up straight, inhabiting herself again. "Everyone is insurance poor," she said, as if she is introducing a PowerPoint. "This is what you have to overcome when you meet a new client, when you walk in the door. You have to smile even though inside you're not even sure you want to sell this policy. But Daddy taught me to put on a game face, and I put on the game face."

Sally thought, *Arthur taught her to do this, to do what he did, hold everything inside. And now she thinks it is strength, but it isn't. It is hardness and sharpness, but it isn't strength. This girl is hard and sharp. I don't want her to break.* But all she did was nod.

"He used to say 'fake it until you make it,'" Fran said. "But lately, I can't fake it and I'm not making it, anymore. Everyone said it's because of 9/11, but you can't go on blaming something that happened to other people for what's happening to you."

"It didn't just happen to other people," Sally whispered. She shouldn't interrupt. She was afraid to contradict.

Fran waved it away. "Maybe it did, maybe it didn't. But I have to be stronger than that. And I don't understand. Business is good, so why is life bad? I'll tell you why. Because Dan can't take the fact that I am doing better than he is, writing more policies."

"Oh, Fran," Sally said. She meant to convey *how sad it is* but Fran shook her head furiously, as if she knew Sally was questioning its truth.

"Believe me, when Dan won regional salesmen of the year, I was ecstatic. But when I won regional, last year and then this year, he acted like a spoiled baby. Last year I blew it off, but this year he wouldn't even come to the awards dinner with me. And everyone in the office knew it. I was mortified."

"Oh, Franny, I didn't know. I'm so sorry."

She continued as if Sally had not spoken. "And then Chris dropped out of school, and then you go and break your ankle jumping into a grave, and I just can't take it anymore. I wish Daddy was here. Whatever the problem, Daddy knew how to deal with it."

This was the Fran Sally was used to, the angry girl with an axe to grind, and complaints to register.

"He did," Sally said. Even when he got cancer. He had worked, all through the chemo, up to his surgery, after his surgery, in the hospital, out of the hospital.

"Once, I asked him how he coped. You know what he said? He said, 'I fold it up and put it in my pocket and get on with business,'" Fran said.

"Yes," Sally said. "And he did. But Franny, I didn't jump into a grave. I was pushed."

Fran is annoyed. "Okay, Mom. Do you want to hear what happened or not?"

"I do," Sally said. "But I didn't jump into a grave."

"Whatever," Fran said. "So, I go to close on a comprehensive policy that Dan and I were working on, that I brought in, I, me, and shared it with him, I said let's do it as a team, and I go to close and I find out that Dan talked the people out of it."

"How did he talk them out of it?" Sally said.

"The husband was yes and the wife was maybe, and I figured out how they could finance the policy with a step-down when the oldest kid is college age, so it would be like an automatic savings account. And I go over to pitch it to them, and I can see something's up. No one is making eye contact, all of a sudden. So finally, I ask what's going on and that's when they tell me they decided not to buy any insurance at all. Instead, they are going to take that money and invest it in their dream, to open a direct mail business in their garage. So when I got my mouth closed, I asked what made them change their mind, and guess what they said? They said they had us guys – actually, Dan – to thank. Then the wife said, I'm quoting, that 'Dan acted more like a life coach than an insurance salesman. He was awesome.'"

"What did he do? What did he say?"

"Well, awesome Dan called them up and told them not to buy the policy. Under the circumstances."

"What circumstances?" Sally said.

"Just what I asked. The husband said Dan said after 9/11 he didn't know if he even believed in insurance anymore. Insurance was an illusion. When you buy insurance, you are betting against yourself. Maybe we ought to all go out and buy ourselves a boat."

Sally thought it was a cogent thought, but she didn't say so. She put her hand on her daughter's, and felt the curled, cold fingers under hers.

"And when I got home and confronted awesome Dan, you know what he said? He said he really felt that way, and was thinking about changing careers. So I said isn't this a little overreaction to your wife making regional? and he said he was proud of me, but it was not something he cared to do anymore. Like I was boasting about a pile of shit and he decided to stop moving his bowels. And just like that, he said he needed to re-think his life and he wanted to do it alone. He needed space. Just like that, twenty-one years, the marriage is over."

And Sally, thinking *nothing is ever just like that,* kept quiet for once and held her daughter's hand.

"One of these days I'm going to lose my game face, and god knows what I'm going to do then. God, I wish Daddy were here."

And then Fran, the child who never cried fell against Sally, and let her enclose her in her arms, and cried again, and cried.

* * *

The cleaning service was finished, so Sally went back to Maiden Lane one more time. She said there were one or two things she wanted to pick up before she handed the keys over to the landlord. "The landlord" was once a middle-aged man in a suit and tie and hat that sat too high on his head, and who had been unsmiling but not impolite, and said "thank you" when she handed him the rent each month. Now, "the landlord" is an entity, a large realty company with a sales division, a leasing division, and she pays in half-yearly increments, all her communication taking place by mail, through and with the entity, and she has never seen a human. But she understands that they were thrilled to be finished with her, and her ridiculous stabilized rent. Now the whole block of space was going to be gutted and re-done.

"What do you have to pick up?" Emily asked.

Sally was vague. "This and that," she said. She didn't say she just wanted to go there one more time. Sit in her old swivel chair if it was still there. Look in the back seat of the red car.

Sally took the Wall Street bus. When she got on, she recognized her old driver, the Russian girl. Ilana. Ilana looked like hell. Her cheek was creased as if she slept on something that dug into her all night; her hair was matted, the brown roots grown out of the blonde color at least two months' worth.

"Oh, hey," Ilana said, her face reddening with pleasure when she saw Sally. "Sally, so to see you good!"

"And you, Ilana," Sally said. "How's it going?" She scanned the bus, for familiar faces. "Any of the old crowd?"

"Nah. They don't travel by me no more, but I seen them and they're all accountants for. 'Cept you, who is now also."

"I'm glad. So, everything okay with you?" She knew something wasn't.

Ilana wobbled her hand in the air. "So and so," she said. Her eyes filled with tears.

"What happened?" Sally said.

"My husband died," Ilana said.

"Oh, dear," Sally said. "Was he downtown?"

Ilana shook her head. "No. That's what everyone ask. He died in the hospital. And people act like he didn't die as dead as everyone else. Or like he was lucky to die of cancer in a bed." Her eyes are red-rimmed. "I don't sleep," she said.

The Wall Street bus was half empty. Sally sat behind Ilana, feeling obliged to stay and hear the rest of the story; there did not seem to be one.

Finally, Sally said, "Have you talked to someone, gotten some help?"

She said no. "The bus company, they had a grievance counselor for a while. But when she found out my husband didn't die *there,*" pointing her thumb out the window, "she said I didn't need to come, no more. I would go through everything natural, not like the others."

"What an idiot," Sally said.

"Right?" Ilana said. "Right?"

Before she got off the bus, Sally handed Ilana Emily's card. "She's a psychologist, and she's got a good heart," Sally said. She was going to say "she's my daughter," but she didn't want it to look like she was drumming up business, which she wasn't. She just wanted to help.

"You have a life to live, Ilana," she said, giving her a little hug.

"You, too, Sally," she said.

Sally got lost. There were still closed streets and she got herself all turned around, and had to stop and ask for directions several times just to find her way back to Maiden Lane. The red car was gone. She walked around the block, as if someone might have moved and re-parked it. She came back around, passing the tax preparer's storefront. The tax preparer himself was inside, at a large metal desk. She opened the door slowly and put her head and shoulders in. The tax preparer looked up and motioned her in. The space was dusty and stacks of books and papers, some as high as the lowest pictures on the wall, covered the floor. The pictures were all beach scenes.

"Mr. Foster, hi, I'm Sally, I used to be your neighbor," she said, "SEASONED GREETINGS, down the block." She was suddenly embarrassed that she had spent all these years avoiding his slightly inquisitive, friendly attention. There were dark circles under his eyes and his jowls sagged, and bits of hair sprouted from his ears.

"Come in, come in," he said. "After all these years."

"Yes, I know, I know, so many years... and then..." Sally said. She didn't know what was left to say.

"So let me ask you this. If nothing happened, would you be here now? If I wasn't the last man on Maiden Lane?"

"Well, of course not," she said, thinking what a shame, she could have been long-time friends with this droll and interesting man.

"Exactly my point," he said. "Life adjusts."

She isn't sure what the point is. "How?"

"I don't know. However."

"I agree with you there," she said, enjoying the nonsense.

"Obviously you weren't here," he said.

"No, were you?"

He shook his head. "Seeing a client uptown. It took me six hours to get home," he said, and then shrugged, as if he saw how unimportant that selfish detail was in the whole scheme of it. But he wanted to claim a piece of the hardship, too.

"Everyone's upset," she said. "How long have you been back?"

"Since a week after," he said.

"Did you see what happened to the red car?"

"What red car?" he said.

It was impossible, but not entirely impossible, her idea about the owner of the red car. It wasn't as if no one else died. And in the Catch-22 world of the city agencies, maybe just because she called the Department of Transportation, they didn't come. Maybe if she had not called them, they would have come in a routine sweep, and walked past the car and noticed the expired registration (had it expired? She had never looked), and looked in the back seat, and seen the baby (if there was one) asleep. But no, they never came and the baby (if there was one) was dead. By the time they came the baby would have been dead. And then they would have looked up the owner of the car, for them it would have been a piece of cake, and they would have found out that the driver had died suddenly, in a hit and run accident just across the street, in front of Duane Reade, and next to the body was a Duane Reade bag with diapers. And they would have contacted the family and discovered that there had been a city-wide alert for the disappearance of the baby and its parent. She cannot tell in her fantasy if the parent was a mother or a father, but it didn't matter. The funeral for the baby took place at the same cemetery where Susie was buried. It was ridiculous but not entirely impossible, just as it was not entirely impossible that a plane had just crashed in Rockaway and the black smoke looked like 9/11 all over again. Nothing was entirely impossible, which is what she was afraid of. And she couldn't get the dead baby out of her mind.

Sally asked CJ to ask her journalist friend to find out the name, address, and telephone number of the owner of the red car. She gave her the plate number. "Journalists have connections," she said.

* * *

Sally didn't have to ask Mark why he was getting a divorce. He and Robin did not get along. They had never gotten along. But they had not split up yet, and of all three of her children, she is surest of him, that he and Robin will go on living together in the same house, fighting over who will get the best television set, and watching the news on it together every evening, fighting over the children, and uniting when the children need them. They would live in misery for sure, but divorce? They were falling short of divorce. "Emily said Dad and I had such a perfect marriage that all you kids can't compete and that's why you're all getting divorced."

Mark had come over to fix the screen door and was instead painting the porch rail. When Sally objected, he said it was dingy looking, and that she had better guard against things getting out of hand. If she ever wanted to sell the thing, he said. *The thing? My home? And do what? Go to Florida, like your in-laws?*

"Hmm," he said. "Perfect? What about that little thing Dad had with Ann?"

"Ann? Are you for real?"

"Around when she helped him out at tax time," he said.

"Mark, I don't know where you come up with these things," she said. Can he be projecting? Did he cheat on Robin with someone in his office, someone he worked with? "Maybe you have cheating on the brain, my boy," she said.

He shook his head, definitely no. "I can be an asshole sometimes, Mom, but one thing I would never do is cheat on Robin. We're in this together. To the end. If it ever comes."

"Will it ever come?" she said. But she means to say, *And your father would?*

With Mark it was always so easy to know what he thinks. He just put it out there. He shrugged. "I don't know. Ever since we said we were getting divorced we've gotten along better. Maybe we just had to threaten each other to realize we don't want to. And then, when everything happened... what's going on in the world... we are just going great. Maybe it made us see what's important."

"And what's that?" Sally said, suddenly sick of him. As if buildings can explode, worlds can change, all in service to him. To teach him and his nutty beauty of a wife a lesson. Make him see the light. What an ego. And in the back of her mind, *Why would he say something like that about his father and my dead friend Ann?*

"Each other," he said, "family," and surprised her by putting down the paintbrush and giving her a hug.

That night, sleepless again, she told Arthur, though he was dead five years, that she wanted a divorce. Maybe that would retroactively clear up some little things that had come between them. Then she took half a pill and slept. Yes.

* * *

Bradley loved fine dining and he enjoyed surprising Sally with a new and wonderful restaurant every time they went out. And while Sally's tastes in food were plainer, the new, or exotic, or expensive, or something-else-special food gave them something to talk about, a reliable topic at the table and during the evening. He spoke knowledgeably about spices and methods of cooking, and Sally enjoyed listening to him. (Though he doesn't cook, himself, he said. He finds it too fraught with accidental occurrences, spills and other variabilities.) She was getting accustomed to Bradley's stiff way of speaking, and tried to think of it as a likeable quirk. In a way, she was reassured by the distance the formality of speech provided. There was no need to be close. So when he asked her to join him on a cruise to the Bahamas, she didn't immediately say no. He proposed it, he said, because of the "single supplement" – a surcharge levied on people who travel alone – and that the two of them together would qualify for the better price, just for being a couple.

"How romantic," Sally said, and Bradley hesitated, and she thought he had finally caught on to her sarcasm, but then he nodded.

After their first kiss there had been no more, and Sally had the pleasant suspicion that Bradley was, like her, free of any interest in sex (with her?) or so satisfied with the first kiss that he would not crave another one for years. Either way, she liked not having to think about it, though she did ask him about their sleeping arrangements, mainly because she figured she should. He assured her he had no "ulterior motives" about "moving up to the next level" but that in order to take advantage of the "price point differential" they would have to indulge in a little subterfuge. In other words, they would have to share a stateroom.

"Let me think about it," she said.

Dr. Joe – just Joe now, he insisted – had gotten into the habit of stopping by the house. He came late, after his rounds at North Shore Hospital. Always without warning. He always said he was just driving by to say hello, just in and out, but Sally inevitably said she has just made a pot of coffee, how about a cup before you go, and there was always a piece of cake, or sometimes she said, "You look hungry," and made him a scrambled egg on a bagel. "Are you sure?" he always said. He liked his bagel toasted, with the excess dough of each half scooped out. Sally made sure she had a dozen scooped out bagel halves in the freezer and she bought real butter when he said he liked it better and it was healthier than that dietetic margarine. She looked forward to these drive-bys. The old ease she had always felt with him, even when he was taking care of Artie, was back. And since he didn't mention anything about taking her "out" on a "date" again, there was nothing in the least stressful or illicit about it. Yet she avoided mentioning his visits to the children and when avoidance became deliberate lies, she had to ask herself why she was so sure that the children would not approve. As surely as they welcomed Bradley, she knew they would not welcome Joe. Knowing it undid her ease, but only a little, because there was something so comforting and pleasurable about watching the late-night news with someone again, that she did not want to give it up. It was innocent and natural, having him there, falling asleep on the leather sofa, snoring lightly, while she sat and watched the muted images until he woke, five or ten minutes later, with a start, took a slug or two of the cooling coffee, saying, "Ahh, that was good," with the soft burr of recent sleep in his voice.

"I don't know how you do that," Sally said.

"All those years of interning, residency, midnight shifts, double shifts..." he said. "The body learns to sleep fast. But throw me out anytime," he said. He didn't want to keep her up.

"You're not," she assured him. "I don't sleep."

"What keeps you up?" he said.

"I should never have retired," she said. To her surprise, she made the admission easily. He was easy to talk to. Talking to him was like having Susie back, in a way. He gets the way she thinks. They talked about everything and nothing. He liked hearing about the greeting card business. It made her remember how interesting it was, digging up sayings, getting ideas. He asked her about how such and such idea came up, how she turned it into a card. He remembered the welcome home from Vietnam card from the sixties, which had been hers. They talked about 9/11. She told him about Ilana, the bus driver, and Mr. Foster, and the red car. She liked the words he used which showed he was paying attention. He never said those catch-all phrases like someone was "in denial," or an event was "devastating" or "incredible." He was real.

He told her he had run down to the ER that day, to help the injured, and there had been no one to help, everyone injured had died. She didn't say, "You must have been devastated," and he didn't say, "I was devastated," or "It was incredible." She was moved to put a sympathetic hand on his arm for a moment.

She loaned him one of her favorite books of short stories and was surprised when a week later he had read it. The stories were by Raymond Carver. She had given it to him because of the one about Chekhov on his deathbed, and how his doctor, instead of sending for oxygen, had ordered champagne.

"Is that what you would have done?" she asked.

He said probably not. "I'm too obsessive," he said. "I would have sent for the oxygen even if I knew it was too late to do any good." She noticed how he rubbed his hands together all the time, as if he were constantly scrubbing in, for a surgery.

"What if Chekhov told you not to?" she said, which is what happened in the story (but not precisely what she meant). He sipped his coffee and rubbed his hands and shrugged. "In that case... I don't know," he said.

She said, "You once told me that you never get used to losing a patient. What do you do to comfort yourself?"

He said, brusquely, "I tell myself you win some, you lose some."

"Are you kidding?"

"No."

He put his hand lightly over hers, and she slid it free, pretending she needed to pick up a napkin, tapping her lips with it.

She talked about Susie, and how she felt when she died, how their secrets evaporated. She had discovered then that a secret isn't a secret unless it is shared by two people, and kept from others.

"I'll tell you a secret," he said. "I never wanted to be a doctor."

"What did you want to be?"

"A veterinarian. I couldn't get into veterinary school, so I settled for med school."

"You better really keep that one a secret," she said. "It's bad for business."

"Your turn," he said. So she told him about Bradley's invitation. He smiled at what he called "the man's inspired practicality."

"What do you think?" she said.

He was picking crumbs off the top of a crumb cake. "I think

you should go," he said.

She flushed. "Really? I don't think I will."

"Why not?"

"I don't want to share an intimate space with him," she said, and even to her own ears it sounded a little evasive, a little prudish.

"What's with you and sex?" he said. "Maybe you *should* 'move up to the next level.'"

"Let's not talk about it," she said. "I'm not comfortable discussing this with you. It's inappropriate." She pulled the crumb cake away from him. "Now who's going to eat it without a top?" she said.

"Don't get huffy, Sally. You brought it up."

"I shouldn't have." But then she blurted out, "The truth is I'm done with sex, Joe. I don't want to start again. I want to stay done with it. Okay?"

"You don't like it, or you don't want it?" he said.

"I don't know," she said. "Both? Both. Can we not talk about this anymore?"

"Is it about old bodies?" he said. "We both have old bodies."

For a moment they both stop breathing. "I mean we all have old bodies. Bradley, you, me..."

She shook her head. "It's too much trouble. It's messy and complicated."

"Oh, for God's sake, Sally, it's not. It's fun," he said.

She didn't want to argue. So she just shook her head again.

"So, what do you want from the man?" he said.

"Friendship," she said. "He's a kind and nice man, and I want us to get to know each other and be good friends."

"I thought that was what *we* were doing," he said. "Brad is another story. He doesn't want to get to know you. He wants to be your *boy*friend. You'll never get away with this friendship stuff with Brad. I think you'd better go on the cruise or cut the man loose."

He covered her hand with his again, large and warm, almost hot from the coffee cup. This time he didn't let her pull away. "As for me, don't worry, I'm fine. But if you should change your mind, you'll let me know?" Then he went home.

Drive-by? That was a hit and run.

A few days later he showed up in the afternoon. "What are you doing?" he said. He had had a bright idea, he wanted her to come with him to the country, to his country house.

"You should have given me some warning," she said.

"I didn't want to," he said. "Give you time to think of an excuse why you can't come." He had groceries in the car. He had already shopped for the overnight.

"Why did you think I would come?" she said.

"I live in hope," he said.

"Well, I'm sorry then," she said. She had a date with Fran the next day. But she made him come in and she used the groceries to cook him a beautiful dinner. And then she promised she would go with him another time.

"When?" he said.

"Let me think about it," she said.

"That's what I wanted to avoid," he said.

* * *

Fran stopped by... "I don't know how to tell you this," Fran said. "Emily is seeing Fred."

Sally was sure she misunderstood. Emily, her baby, barely forty, is seeing her neighbor, Fred, the man who dressed up like an ape because it passed the time. Twenty years her senior. "What do you mean by 'seeing'?" she said.

"What do you think I mean?" Fran said.

Sally put her hand over her mouth. "I can't stand it," she said. She wanted to throw up, but at the same time it struck her as funny, the way the last thing in a long list of things gone wrong can strike you as funny even when it's not: spilt milk, late for work, splinter, slip on the icy sidewalk, paper cut... then a fender bender. And at that point you have to laugh and say to someone "what a day" or "what a week" or "what a year." Emily with Fred was the fender bender.

"Are they having an affair?" she said.

"An *affair?*" Fran squeaked. "How sophisticated."

"Don't correct my English, Fran," Sally said. "Are they sleeping together?"

The answer was yes. Fender bender? This was a car wreck. Oh God. Sally thought of Fred's hairy legs, which she knew from many a backyard party. What must the rest of him be like? Oh God. And Emily was thinking of moving in with him.

There are the obvious questions. "When did this happen? Do you think it is a rebound thing? How could this have happened? How did you find out? What are we going to do?" None of the questions were sensible.

Why was no one talking about the aesthetics of these things? Was Sally the only one who noticed Fred's hairy legs? And what about his thighs? And the other thing?

She went out to get the mail and saw a couple standing on Fred's lawn and did not know them until the woman of the couple waved and called her Mom. When Emily came into the house a while later, Sally was in the shower. They talked to each other from either side of the bathroom door, and finally, Emily said she would drop by later to talk and then she left. When Sally heard the front door slam, she got out of the shower.

The next day she spied Emily kissing Fred. They were leaning against his Simonized car. She watched for as long as she could and then she closed the blinds.

Emily came inside. Sally smiled at her.

Emily said, "Mom, what's wrong with your face?"

She said, "Nothing. I'm smiling. How are you?" Thinking how can one little changed detail of a daughter's life make her as much a stranger as some stranger from Milwaukee? "I heard it from the grapevine," Sally said.

"Hoo hoo. Hoo hoo," Emily said. "Well, it's true."

Looking for the right words for things has been Sally's preoccupation as well as her occupation all her life. She was devoted to her sayings. What was there to say about this? *This too shall pass?* The drunkard's prayer about accepting what you can't change? Instead, she stuttered, "What? I mean how..."

"I don't know, " Emily said. "But I'm happy."

"There's a poem by Kenneth Koch..."

"Oh, Mom, for God's sake," Emily said.

"One Train..."

Emily was not going to listen. She got up and started for the door.

"Don't go, Em," Sally said. "I want you to stay."

"Then stop talking about it like it's a disease you have to cure," she said. "I'm in love."

Sally nodded as if she agreed, all the time thinking of what she could say that wouldn't sound like it was something you had to cure, a saying that would, actually, cure it. She thought so hard that for a moment she forgot what she was thinking about. Then she remembered. "What do you have in common? What do you talk about?" she said.

They talked about everything. It seems Fred was an interesting man. A funny man. He knew about economics, and politics, and jazz.

"Jazz?" Or was the question what did Emily care about economics and politics and jazz?

His daughter, Marcie, had no problem with it, Emily said. Why did Sally?

Well of course Marcie had no problem with it. With Emily around she didn't have to look after her father. She probably preferred him dating her childhood friend to him dressing up like a gorilla.

"The whole family is disintegrating," Sally said.

"No, we're not, we're reconfiguring."

While Emily went to make tea, Sally went to the bookcase and found the poem. When she came back, Sally had her finger in the place. "Listen to this," she said, quickly, before Emily could object. "One train may hide another train/That is, if you are waiting to cross/The tracks, wait to do it for one moment at/ Least after the first train is gone." When she looked up to see how Emily was taking it, the room was empty.

"I mean maybe someone better is just around the corner," she said, anyway.

Around Thanksgiving, Sally told Bradley she would go with him on a cruise, but Bradley had had a change of heart. He had too much work to do "at present," so he could not take a cruise "at this time." She suspected it was a little too much for him. She was not offended. He took her to a new restaurant that served Vietnamese food, as a consolation prize, she thought. He introduced her to his daughter, who had a precise way of speaking, too.

"I guess that means you're a couple," Mark said.

"I suppose," she said. "A little. For now."

After the New Year someone wrote an article about the fact that the air in lower Manhattan was still full of human dust.

* * *

A February birthday was always good for a party. New Year was gone, and Super Bowl, and everyone had settled into that sun-deprived state that some marketer called SAD so he could sell a lamp.

Sally was cataloging her recipes and every three or four she found one she wanted to try again, so her freezer was full and she was looking forward to all the fuss of emptying it onto platters and trays. The children, grandchildren, Fred, of course, were coming, and his daughter, Marcie. She invited Bradley and his daughter, who was bringing one of her children.

And at the last minute, she invited Joe, who might or might not make it. Nevertheless, she prepared the children for his coming, with some semblance of the truth: *Dr. Joe is a friend of Brad's; I run into Dr. Joe when I take Aunt Rita to the doctor.* And then, it looked like he wasn't going to show. Halfway through the party, Rita asked if he was coming, and Sally pretended she didn't even remember if she had asked him or not.

When everyone arrived, Emily pulled the big wing chair covered in red poppy linen into the center of the living room, and told Sally to sit there, because they had a surprise for her. For her birthday, the children and grandchildren had put together a book in her honor. In it were testimonials from each of them, personal anecdotes illustrating some of her best sayings, with commentary, which they were going to read to her now. Sally, who suspected something was up, was delighted and touched, and with a mock-queenly gesture she told them to go ahead, have at it. The book had a big photo of Sally when she was about fifty, on the front cover, under the title, Grandma's Little Book of Big Sayings. She remembered now when CJ coaxed her into looking at family pictures. She must have stolen it then so they could blow it up.

"It's so professional looking!" Sally said.

"That's Robin," Mark said. (His wife was a graphic artist. Robin smiled for a change.)

Emily read the introduction. "Written by me," CJ said, raising her hand. *Looking for the right words for things has been Sally Battel's occupation as well as her preoccupation, all her life. She is devoted to her sayings. The things she wrote in her greeting cards were things she lived by. She believed in them. We think if she didn't write them down, she could not live them.*

Sally thought this was true to an extent, though the way it was written made her sound a bit rigid about it. "Am I that rigid?" she said, and everyone said, "No, of course you're not." But it was certainly true. The things you say about the things you do, matter. Words count. *And every one of us has his or her favorite saying to live by. Presenting our favorites. The top five to stay alive.*

Everyone clapped, and Mark whistled through his two fingers.

Fran went first. "My best of Mommy's sayings is *put things in perspective.* When I had a problem, she tried to make me see the big picture. (Even though I thought my problem WAS the big picture.) Like when Dougie had colic, I thought I'd lose my mind and Mom kept saying *keep it in perspective,* babies aren't colicky at five, or ten, or fifteen, it's only while they are getting used to the world. She's telling me this while he's wailing his head off. I swear I didn't believe her, I wanted to kill her. But she was right. Now Dougie is my most reasonable child."

Sally remembered coming into Fran's apartment, hearing Douglas wailing, and following the sound to the bedroom, where Fran, disheveled, desperate, was holding the baby away from her, her arms stretched out, as if she were about to drop him, or throw him. Sally kept talking to her softly as she reached for the baby, peeling her daughter's fingers from the baby's little body, pretending she did not see where the marks remained, pretending not to know what was in her daughter's mind. She remembered not trusting her to be alone with the baby, engineering it so she or Artie, or someone else be with her as often as she could, or taking Dougie overnight, for almost a year. And she had never told another soul what she saw, and what she understood it to mean.

Mark said, "When I was in little league, I got beaned by a baseball, and I wanted to quit, and Mom wouldn't let me. She said, *It isn't what happens to you, it's what you make of what happens to you, that counts.* She wanted me to use the experience to learn how to take a licking and keep on ticking."

"But that's not what happened," Sally said. "I wanted you to use it to learn to lose gracefully. To lose without losing it. But you used it to work so hard at baseball that you didn't lose."

This was true. And Sally had learned to leave Mark's fury alone. His fury was his strength, and trying to curb it would be like cutting Samson's hair.

"But I still used it," Mark said. "That's the point, isn't it? Except..." then he sang two bars of "My Way."

Rita said her favorite was, *Concentrate on the point of pain.*

Sally got that from yoga, when you do a pose and take it to the nth point and then you can dissipate the pain just by focusing on it. She had done a lot with that. She could cure her own headache. She made Artie do it when he was very sick. He said it helped him. He said it was as good as morphine, sometimes. "I do it, sometimes and it works," Rita said. Sally hugged her, and tried not to think about how frightened she sounded.

CJ said her favorite was *you earn your face.*

"Granny always said if you don't smile, you'll get frown lines. If you're going to get any lines at all, make sure they go up. If they don't, it's your own fault."

Douglas liked the one about *Tell me something wonderful.*

Sally hugged her sad sack grandson, thinking that of all of them, it hadn't worked on him. He used to try so hard. He would say, in desperation, "I didn't throw up this morning, Grandma," and then look at her anxiously, to see if she would accept it as something wonderful. Of course, she always did, clapping and laughing, because it was funny, how hard he tried, and how wonderfully sweet he was.

His brother, Matt, who was away at school and couldn't come in for the party, said his favorite of Grandma's sayings was, *Don't be a victim of your own life.*

Sally looked up, surprised. "Did I say that?" she said, and everyone laughed. "Why would I have said that to Matt? What in his young life could he have been in danger of being a victim of?"

"Me," Fran said.

"Oh, God, Franny, no," Sally said, but then everyone laughed again, and Fran said lighten up, she was kidding.

Everyone was in a circle around Sally. They held paper plates of all the goodies she had made, salad and lasagna and slices of quiche in their laps, wine glasses nearby, raised and lowered and raised and sipped again as she was toasted after each little reading. It was a nice party and Sally was having a very nice time, pleased at the surprise, pleased that her food was being eaten and she was being appreciated.

"My very favorite of Mom's sayings is, "You can't go east all your life and end up in the west," Emily said. "It has a poetic vibe."

And Joe walked in. He waved at Sally from the front door. He was wearing jeans and an electric blue cashmere sweater, and he slipped in and stood beside Brad. "Don't let me interrupt," he said. So Emily said, again: "You can't go east all your life and end up in the west."

Of course, she is thinking of herself, and of this crazy, ridiculous new love object, Fred. But out of the blue, Sally thought of Artie, her Artie, who was east. And wondered how she could find herself unexpectedly, at her age, way out west. In an intemperate, more than nice, wild west in electric blue cashmere and boots.

Rita patted her hand. "Are you all right?" she said. "You're all red and flushed."

Later, after Brad and his family left, and Rita was up in Sally's room lying down, Joe sat down with Sally and her kids, "It's been a long time, Dr. Joe," Emily said.

They were sitting in the added-on front room with the skylight (the "den"), and a cold February sun barely lit the room. Mark put the lights on.

"It has, Emily," he said.

73

You didn't have to be a psychologist to read the scene. The body language was clear. Emily's arms were folded across her chest. Mark's were behind his back; and Fran, the least subtle of the three, turned her back and was looking out the window.

Joe, on the other hand, looked relaxed, but Sally noticed he was drywashing his hands like he was preparing to do surgery.

"How about something to drink?" Sally said. "Mark, there's another bottle of Chardonnay in the fridge. Or an open bottle of Pinot on the counter."

"I'll have a scotch if you have any," Joe said.

"Happens I do," Sally said, and the fact that they had bought it together and he knew and she knew and the others didn't know, made it their secret. She smiled. He stopped rubbing his hands together.

It was Fran who moved things along. "So, Dr. Joe," she said, "You must carry a shitload of malpractice insurance."

Mark, who was in the middle of sipping his beer, choked. Emily uncrossed her arms and covered her mouth, and Rita, who had just wandered into the room, fell back onto the sofa as if someone pushed her.

"I do," Joe said. "Why do you ask?"

"My sister wants to sell you some more," Mark said, and everyone laughed.

The evening deepened but the party kept going in a quiet, sleepy way.

"I've invited your mother to the country, to my country house, " Joe said.

Emily wanted to know where the house was. She had re-folded her arms, but now she was sitting down and had uncrossed her legs.

"Rhinecliff," Joe said. "Near Woodstock."

"Mom, isn't that where you and Daddy once had a house?" Fran said.

"Not far," Sally said. "We were in Red Hook. You were born

by then, Fran."

"I have no memory of it," Fran said. "How come you sold it?"

"Your Dad didn't want to. I hated it, though. Not the house, the house was cute. But the up and back, the traffic every weekend, having to remember to take this and that and shopping for two pantries and two refrigerators. It shortened the weekend by half a day each way. I had to leave work early Friday and get in late Monday."

"What would it have been worth today? If you had kept it in the family," Mark said "God, I don't want to think about it."

She hoped he was not going to start ranting about his father's over-cautiousness about money matters. Or how selling it and missing out on this profit was all her fault, because she pushed his father around. Or why his father had not looked far enough into the future to see how valuable a property it would be thirteen years after they sold it and five years after his death and when his son could have used yet one more infusion of quick cash? Was it money Mark needed?

"Well..." she sighed

"Hindsight," Rita said.

For a moment it looked as though Mark was going to argue, but then Joe said, "Tell me, Mark, are you in real estate? You sound very knowledgeable."

"No, but I study the markets," he said. And then he launched into trends and markets, and the dangerous moment was over.

Part II

Afternoon: Reconfigurations

Sally went with Joe to his house in Rhinecliff. He included Brad in the invitation, but Brad declined, saying he had work to catch up on.

Joe drove out from the city to pick her up late in the day. He had a bagful of groceries, and a lamp in the back of the car, which he transferred to the trunk to make room for Sally's overnight, and by the time they got on the road, it was tipping into rush hour. Before he arrived, while she was waiting for him to arrive, she was planning to cancel. She would suggest they wait and go another time, when they could get an earlier start, or when Brad could make up the threesome. But then there he was, full of enthusiasm, wearing a driving cap and how could she say no?

Once he was there, in her presence, the slight reservation she always had about him when they were apart went away.

She remembered the drive to her and Artie's old house. "I'm not going to say 'it feels like yesterday' anymore, I think I say it too much," she said, as they go over the Whitestone Bridge.

"It's our age," he said. "It's what we're experiencing every day."

She said he seemed to take aging in his stride. He was almost ten years older than Sally, but he didn't act like it bothered him.

"I don't like to complain," he said.

"I do," she admitted, smiling. "It's one of my favorite things."

He took his hand off the wheel to pat her hand, which was lying in her lap. "Yes you do, Sally," he said, laughing. "It's one of the things I love about you."

She could feel herself blush. "Well, then I'll have to complain a lot more," she said.

"Okay, start with why you didn't like the country."

"I felt like an outsider. Not only downstater against upstater, but Jew against gentile. I mean you ride along 9W, along the Hudson, there's miles and miles of monasteries and retreat houses and religious orders, Brothers this and Saint that and

Christian something else. God, I never felt more Jewish. And I didn't like it."

"What's wrong with feeling Jewish?"

"I have no problem *being* Jewish. I just don't want to have to *feel* affiliated with anything, because I'm not. I never go to temple, I never want to, and I didn't like the feeling that I would have to identify myself as a Jew just to make sure everyone knew I wasn't a Christian."

"And say something about Jews you might not want to hear?"

"Probably. But I didn't parse it out, then. I just knew I felt like a lamb out of water."

He laughs. "You mean a fish."

"What did I say?"

"You said 'a lamb out of water,'" he said.

"Did I? Well, lamb to the slaughter, fish out of water."

"Lamb to the slaughter is you?"

"Absolutely," she said, hoping he would take it as the joke she half-meant it to be. "Going away with a strange man... to a secluded house in the gentile woods..."

"I'll try not to take advantage," he said. "I'll try and make it worth your while."

"Well, you better," she said. And all at once she was relieved, as if they had settled something.

The weekend traffic on the Taconic was at a standstill and they stopped talking while he concentrated on driving, shifting lanes, on the shoulder, weaving in and out until they had passed what turned out to be an overheated car. She found herself scanning the road for red cars, and shook her head a little, as if she could shake the thought loose and throw it away. She even opened the window a bit, to let it fly. She forced her attention back to the traffic and the way Joe threaded his way down the road: quick, aggressive. The word sexy came to mind, but in the way they use the word these days, in the ad business, not really about sex.

"Arthur used to curse at drivers like you," she said.

When traffic eased, they talked again. He asked about Mark. "What's he got against you?" he said. "Why does he go at you the way he does?"

"Because he doesn't believe I'm the real me. He thinks if he rubs me hard enough the shine will come off and the other me will emerge."

"And what will she be?"

"The screaming bitch of his adolescence. He was the only person who ever made me... who can bring the screaming bitch to life. And he misses her and wants her back." Until this moment she had never thought that, and yet now she knew it was true.

He admitted to her that he had invited his son and wife to come down from Albany to meet her.

"And you're telling me now?"

"Would you have come if I told you before?"

"You have a point," she said. "What time are they coming?" she asked. He shrugged. "Sometime tomorrow. Whenever the wife tells him to come, they'll come," he said. She noticed he called his daughter-in-law "the wife" and wondered why he didn't like her.

"You'll see," he said.

"I bet you told them I was your girlfriend," she said.

"What if I did?" he said.

The house was at the top of a mountain and all the walls were windows. You could see far and wide: clouds, trees, setting sun, rocky steeps, mountains flat and wide, crouching in front of higher and higher peaks, like the shortest kids in a class picture; in the background, the highest, which she guessed was Overlook; and in the distance, like the superlative in a long list of comparatives, the Hudson. She felt glassed in, bullied, pressed by the magnitude and extreme beauty. She put a frame around it, like the painter, Thomas Cole had done: that is the

Hudson down there. It was so cold she was shivering. What is so beautiful about that? "Why do they call the Hudson beautiful?" she said.

"The curves," Joe said. "The way the river curves, like a woman."

He put the heat up and turned on all the lights. He went out to the shed for logs for a fire. "Bringing the house back to life," he said. "I love the ritual."

She liked this. "If I had thought that way, we never would have sold the house. Damned nuisance, I used to think, starting over every time."

He gave her the guest bedroom and he took the master bedroom. There was another bedroom for his son and his wife. While she changed, he put the food away and poured them drinks. His son had e-mailed that he was coming in the morning. So, they had the evening. They decided not to go out for dinner but to cook what he brought for tomorrow's lunch, instead: a pound of shrimp, French bread, brie, an avocado, salsa, nuts and a chocolate cake from some fancy bakery in Queens. She cooked and he built a fire in the fireplace. He opened two snack tables and they ate by the fire, and by the time the meal was done, she was relaxed, warm and a little drunk. The room was neat and neutral, with a large, bright abstract painting above the sofa, and an afghan and some pillows the only two splashes of color.

"Did your wife decorate the room?"

Joe nodded. "Everything but the pillows and the afghan. She said pillows and blankets belong in the bedroom, period."

He turned on the television, and they watched the news, then flipped around the channels looking for something. They found an old Woody Allen movie, called *The Front*, about the McCarthy era.

She had been recently out of college, working for a small-time music publisher. "Manny Gedalter. Love Music. The Brill

Building on 47th Street, where Irving Berlin used to have an office. I wanted to be a songwriter once," she said. She had loved being around all the Tin Pan Alley types, a lot of them eastern European immigrants, who grew up on socialism and unionism. Not serious communists. "Pinkos, they called them." Gedalter had made piles of money in the fur business and then gambled it all in music. He loved musicians. Published songs for Eddie Cantor, Sophie Tucker, Frank Sinatra, Dick Haymes. He could hear a song once and know it would be a hit. He got the Inkspots their first hit. "He called them *the schvartzers.*"

"What was their famous song?" Joe asked.

They can't remember.

"Anyway, one day someone from Local 802, the musicians' union, came around with a petition against McCarthy and Manny wasn't there so I signed his name for him. Then a week later some FBI people came and asked him questions. I felt terrible."

"If I Didn't Care," Joe said. "The name of the song."

"Yes." She hadn't thought about this in years. She never told Manny it was she who signed the petition and caused him all that trouble.

"What happened to him?"

"He moved out of the Brill Building. To California. Became a very rich producer of jingles."

"Happy ending, then," Joe said.

"Well, yes, but not exactly my point," she said. "I didn't own up."

"Would you do it differently now?" he said.

She thinks and answers honestly. "Yes. Not that I'm a better person. But at least I understand how bad it is to give in to fear."

"People don't necessarily improve with age," Joe said. "And fear..."

She agreed. That was a time of such fear, of the government, of the other. "Like now, in a way. Then it was communists, now it's terrorists. We excuse all kinds of awful behavior in the name of our fear."

"And what's worse, it goes from terrorist, to Muslims in general. Look at those people who don't want a mosque near Ground Zero."

She admitted that to this day she did not sign petitions because of the fear left over from the McCarthy era. She joined the Women Strike for Peace back then, but whenever they asked her to sit outside Bloomingdales to get signatures, or walk a picket line or rally, she made excuses and didn't go. She was too scared.

He said his wife had been part of the Women Strike for Peace, too. "I don't think she was scared of anything."

She felt a pang of jealousy and said it was a wonderful way to be.

"Well, I don't know how wonderful it was," he said. "It could be tough to live with. When she was diagnosed with breast cancer, she took it better than I did. She accused me of expecting a free pass because I was an oncologist. She was right. I was pissed off. Once, when they couldn't schedule her chemo session when we wanted it, I went nuts. She told me to bite the bullet. That's the way she was all the way down the line. She was not an emotional person and I had hated it all our life together, but when she was dying, it made her interesting.

"From her point of view, the end-of-life decision was a no brainer. She wanted no heroic measures. No artificial tricks to run the clock, as she put it. When she sensed she was close to the end, she called Evan, told him to come down and see her, said her goodbye to him and sent him back to school with instructions not to come flying back should she expire. Which she did. The next day."

"I admire that," Sally said. "But that doesn't mean she wasn't frightened. It just means she did it anyway."

That is the moment when it would have made sense to bring

up Arthur and his end-of-life decision, and to ask Joe if he had, but before she could frame the question, the moment passed. "The Front" ended, the late news came on, they had decaf and chocolate cake, then watched a long infomercial called "The Johnny Carson Years."

Sally had her feet up on the sofa, and Joe rubbed her ankles. She did not object.

"Here's a truth," she said. "I've never had a massage. Can you believe it?"

"Incredible," he said. "Why?"

"I just didn't. Never had the time. Never felt the need. Or desire." She felt herself flush at the word. "And, to be completely honest, I felt funny about some stranger putting hands on my bare skin. And giving me pleasure."

He shook her toe. "Did you think you would fall in love with the masseur? Or he with you?" he said.

"I think I thought I would have to. Don't look at me like I have three heads, Joe. Wasn't this the way girls were raised in our day? Wasn't your wife that way? How many women of our generation went for massages?"

He didn't answer but he nodded, granting her the point. He slid a finger between her toes.

"I don't know what your story is with physicality, but I think you're a very warm and sensual woman," he said.

"I'm in the temperate zone," she said. "Really. That's the way I've been most of my adult life. Not cold and not hot. I don't want the high highs and I don't hit the low lows. And you can't be temperate all your life and suddenly not be. You can't travel east all your life and end up in the west. Contentment is more my territory." Then they kissed.

"Open your mouth," he said, talking against her lips.

She opened her mouth and the kiss floored her. She was shaking. He was shaking too.

Arthur's lips had been home, his touch just like hers. It

could have been her own hand he touched her with. With this man – the temperature, the pressure, the design of it, a slight application of pressure – was different. His whole hand was on her back, firmly, she could feel the thumb separating itself, slowly moving outward and back, the whole hand sliding two vertebrae higher, the thumb separating again, making her weak. She was dizzy. He took his hand away and where it had been felt heated. Her body was dissolving, the heat melting her insides.

"If I give myself to you..." she said.

"Then what?" he said.

But she was so dizzy she couldn't think, she didn't know what she meant to propose, and it was too late anyhow. Her clothing was on the floor, his big, warm hands were all over her, she felt his warm, smooth skin, tasted it, as she put her teeth against his shoulder, felt his breath on her, his weight on her. His penis was a tight fit. She made a sound and he stopped and pulled back, making space between them, but she licked her hand and ran it over his penis, bringing him back to her, sliding him inside her. He made love to her with care and passion, and she made love to him intemperately, loudly, a little madly. Afterward, they petted and kissed and then made love again, and she bled a little. "I scraped you up," he said.

"I don't mind," she said.

He hugged her so hard she couldn't breathe but still did not pull away.

"Cunt is not a bad word," she said. "It's middle English."

"Is it," he said.

"How did you know I would be... like this?"

He didn't speak for a few minutes, just smoothed her hair and the sides of her face. "One night, late, I was leaving the hospital to go home, and I stopped in to see Arthur. You were there, and I almost came in, but then I saw his blanket was off, and you were stroking him, trying to bring him off. You were wearing your coat."

She had been ready to leave, to go home, and Arthur had asked her. She had hurried, she had not wanted to "get caught" and she had not liked it, she had wanted it to be over, there were thoughts and smells and sounds that she wanted to be gone, but in some perverse way, it had excited her, and it had made Arthur happy for the moment. "I remember that night," she said.

"And after that, I dreamed about you. Like this – " he ran his hand over her naked body – "with me. I dreamed about you all the time. Your hands, your beautiful eyes, the way you hold your head, the way you touched him."

He called his son and told him not to come. That he had an emergency and had to go back to the city early in the morning. He lied awkwardly and she thought his son must know that they wanted to be alone. She wondered if he had lied awkwardly on purpose, to let him know, wink, wink, or if he was just a bad liar.

They slept in his bed. She didn't sleep. She kept thinking what if his son decided to come and had a key and let himself into the house and found them like this, asleep in each other's arms, with her flat, deflated breasts pressed to his daddy's chest like spilt milk. Or awake, with his hands on them, his mouth on them, her legs wrapping and unwrapping him.

About 4 a.m. he got up to go to the bathroom. When he came back, he came around to her side of the bed and sat on the edge. She got alarmed; something was wrong. He said, tentatively, would she mind... *This is a mistake, this is a mistake,* her mind was racing. But it was only that she was on his side of the bed. Would she mind rolling over to the other side? His side was warmer and the sheets were not so scrambled. You're a tidy sleeper, she said. He took her hand and held it as if they were in a high wind. They were both wide awake. He put on the radio, but they couldn't get anything but BBC and after a while they turned it off.

"If you gave yourself to me... What?" he said.

"You'd have to promise not to give me back," she said.

Eventually, she fell asleep, and when she woke, for a moment she didn't know what bed she was in, in what house, in what town, in what day, in what year. She began to perspire and her heart was beating so fast and loud she thought the man had to be able to hear it and she put her hand to her chest to quiet it. When he asked her if she wanted toast or cereal she answered with his suddenly retrieved name. Joe. Joe. The cereal, or the way she woke up, gave her indigestion for half the rest of the day.

He told her this: He was married to his wife, Julia, just starting out, still in medical school. His son had not been born yet. He came home from work early and saw a man he knew leaving his apartment. His wife at the time stood at the door and saw the man off. It was clear to Joe that there was intimacy between them. His wife had kissed the man goodbye. The man had touched his wife's breasts. He did not just know this man. This man was his close friend, his cadaver partner. This man was engaged to be married himself, to a nurse at the hospital. He did not say anything to his wife. He never said a word but for years he took small revenges on both of them. What kind of revenges? He "forgot" his wife's birthday that year and their anniversary, too. He pretended he was having an affair. Well, not all the revenges were small. When he became chief of oncology and had a chance to hire this man, a fairly decent doctor, though not a great one, he didn't. This was years later. The guy got a job elsewhere and did not suffer. When his wife got pregnant, just a few months after this happened, Joe was afraid that the boy was not his own. It was only because Evan looked exactly like him that the fear went away.

"Did you ever forgive her?"

"Eventually."

"I don't know that I would ever. If Arthur had cheated on

me."

There was a small silence.

"Am I sure he didn't?" she said.

"Yes. Are you sure?"

She nodded. "Absolutely. I once told him that if I found out he was cheating, I would know it was only sex and I wouldn't care. We were best friends."

"Was that true?"

She shook her head. "No. I would have cared very much." She wondered if being honest with Joe meant she was betraying Arthur. Cheating on him.

Joe said no.

"You mean not always?"

"I mean 'no.'"

"How can it be so black and white?"

"Because he is dead and can't be betrayed."

"All right, then, betray his memory."

"That's sentimental. His 'memory' as you call it, is your memory, in your mind and the only way you can betray your own memory is to lie to yourself. He can't be lied to anymore."

"What do you mean 'anymore'? I never lied to him."

Silence.

"So, you mean in all those long years I had to have lied to him?"

Silence.

"I used to buy things and sneak them into the house and then when he asked me if it was something new, I used to tell him I had it for a long time. I even scolded him for not being more attentive to what I wore," she admitted.

The thing was, the truths she was telling didn't really matter. Not that they were lies. But they were not her real secrets. Here was a real secret: when Fran was first born, Sally almost threw her out of the window. It was probably post-partum depression, but she never told anyone. And she was addicted to diet pills at some point. And one day shortly before Artie died, she had felt such rage (what could it have been about?) that she drove into a woman's car door, ripping it off its hinges. She had said of course, to the insurance company, to Artie, to the children, to everyone, that the woman opened the door suddenly, that she didn't see her. But all the time she knew what had happened. Now, Fran was the one who was always getting angry, with Sally, with her children, with her husband, who was divorcing her or the other way around. Did Fran have an infant memory of almost being thrown out the window? Did her molecules remember? What Sally really wanted to know about Joe was a secret, too. She wanted to ask him; she had always wanted to know whether he had ever killed anyone.

She offered a semi-secret. "I used to feel superior to my divorced friends." In the middle of life, during the so-called crises everyone was having, she had hung on while they had let go. She had given herself top scores for this. Now, it didn't matter whether they were divorced or she was widowed, they were all in the same boat, and that annoyed her, how the field had suddenly been leveled by time. She had been doing so well, continuing on, weathering marriage the long way, while the others had done it easy, quitting when things got tough, living mini-lives, sub-lives, alter-lives? Her way was the product of harder work, having better character, being better, and yet here they were, completely even, a total wash. It wasn't fair.

She said this while they were walking in the woods. She was wrapped in a poncho that was in the living room closet. When she asked if it were his wife's he said no and then yes. It smelled of something that was popular years ago. *L'Interdit*, maybe, or *L'air du temps*. Something blonde and ladylike.

It had been a long time since she had gone hiking. "I don't think I ever thought about where I put my foot, or what would happen if I misstepped," she said. "Who thought about things like that? Who thought about getting lost, or overheated, or…"

"Are you all right?" Joe said.

"I'm fine," she said. "I'm just saying."

"Do you want to go back?"

"Why? Do you?" she snapped. It irritated her that he could read her so well.

"No. But if you are uncomfortable..."

"Listen," she said, smiling tightly. "Do me a favor, don't read my mind. I'm fine. And by the way, 'uncomfortable' is when you sit on a hard chair. It is not when you ache from a recently sprained ankle, or are frightened of predators and or want to get out of the woods which I'm not and I don't." *Why was she so mad? How did she get so mad?*

They walked on a while without talking, except Joe now and then saying they would turn back soon, until she realized that they were lost. He didn't deny it.

"I didn't want to make you nervous," he said, sheepishly. "Anyway, all roads lead out, eventually."

The woods got denser and then finally thinned out and led to the road. "See?" he said, but she sensed that he was relieved, too. All the time they were walking, she felt they were being followed by a bear. She told him this (hoping it would explain why she snapped at him earlier). "Mark said my worry skills are honed to a sharp edge," she said.

He laughed. "Sons," he said. "Evan calls me 'the mannequin.' He doesn't like the way I dress."

She didn't like it either, but she didn't like his son for criticizing him.

He seemed to have forgotten her sudden flare up, and as they walked back to his house, they stopped and leaned against trees to kiss, like kids. By the time they got back they were both exhausted. The day that had begun cool, and gotten warm, was chilly again. Joe took a hot shower to get warm, and Sally took a book into the living room, but her eyes closed, and half an hour later, when she woke and peeked into the bedroom, Joe was fast asleep. They had reservations at a restaurant in the nearby town, but he slept through them, and at about eight, she sliced an onion and cracked some eggs and put together a light meal. When it was almost ready, she went in to wake him. He didn't apologize for sleeping through dinner or making her put together a makeshift meal, he acted as if this was the best, planned, outcome. He breathed in the cooking and said, "Ahhh" with such pleasure she got a lump in her throat. "Omelets are beautiful," he said, and though she barely tolerated such high-flying food talk and thought it was pretentious nonsense when Brad talked it, she suddenly felt it was exactly true. Omelets were beautiful. Leftover rounds of French bread toasted to a crunch were beautiful, too. A nice stick of butter, beautiful. Onions? Strawberries? Could they be any more gorgeous? She told herself to cut the bullshit, pull the plug, detach the wires, cut the feed. But something wonderful *had* happened, and who was she to deny that it had, or could, or ever would again?

Joe called the restaurant, and didn't lie, saying something had come up, as she might have done, or Artie. "I slept right through our reservation," he said, laughing at himself. She loved that, too.

They turned in early, and he was asleep again almost instantly. But Sally lay awake, trying to read, listening to his funny clicky snore, trying not to want so much for him to wake and kiss her. She thought it was silly, silly, falling in love after a certain age, just silly, having to go through the emotional fuss and bother of it, to endure the awkwardness, having to bare her old, wrinkled, slipping down body to a stranger. How could someone say she was beautiful, a body like hers? Really. She knows what she knows. Did he understand she had gallstones? Did she want to know if he had an upper plate? What would he do when she had gastric upsets? What would she do if he got hair on the soap? But last night everything changed. She was turned on, turned around. She had never been the way she was last night. It was overwhelming, unbearable, magnificent. But then, oh God, she thought, *what if I get sick and can't see it through*, what if he gets sick and dies? It was a terrible risk. "I think it best we don't see each other," she said, and then she imagined he was awake and had heard her, and imagined his eyes, filled with surprise, hurt...

"Oh, Joe, no," she said, and began to cry herself, and put her arms around him, waking him. She said she had a dream that woke her.

So he held her tight. "I want to tell you..." he said. His voice, so recently wakened, sounds hoarse.

"I wanted to tell you... something... since we first met," he said.

"Met now, or then?"

She was not aware if the sound that he made was an answer to her question, or just the rush of air as their bodies came together. **Sunday mornings** had always been Sally's favorite time. In the early days, she had put Artie in charge of the children; when the kids were older, she and Artie both slept in, from Saturday night parties with neighbors, or a late movie, or dinner at Cinque Terre on Parsons Boulevard. After that, Artie was deep into golf, or football games or baseball and she learned to love her Sunday time alone. Artie called it her "woolgathering time."

She woke in Joe's bedroom, in Joe's bed, feeling whiplashed, still dizzy from the unexpected turn her life had taken, and a little bruised. Her lips felt bruised, and between her legs, and she thought she might be charley horsed from the unaccustomed activity. But bruised, too, by the emotionality of it all. One part of her felt it was too much, too much, and she wished she were home already. Joe was quiet, too, and since the day was damp and cool, her suggestion that they head home early did not sound unfriendly. He asked her if she would come again soon. If she would, he would put the leftover stuff into the freezer and the refrigerator and the cupboard. Otherwise, he'd bring it home. She didn't really know, but she said she would. She was wearing the woolly poncho because nothing else was warm enough. "Wear it home," he said. "You look pretty in it." He nuzzled her neck. "And you smell good, too."

"It's your late wife's perfume you're smelling," she said. She would take it home, and dry-clean it. Twice, if she had to. "Was there another woman after your wife?" she said.

"Not really," he said. "No."

"Not really?" she said, thinking of the thin blonde at the dinner dance.

But he didn't answer. Maybe he didn't hear her.

The local radio station said traffic was moderate "on the nines" which means 9W, 9G and 9. "What'dya say? Take 9W down?" Joe said.

It was the long way, but it avoided the Thruway most of the way, so she agreed. They rode silently for a little while.

"Say something," he said.

"I had a nice time," she said. "You?"

He nodded. "Nice hardly covers it, but yes." Then he hesitated. "You asked me... I have been with other women," he said. "I enjoy going out. But I have never been with someone like you."

While she was thinking of asking what "someone like you" actually meant, the words began to crumble into sounds and then she was asleep.

They are on a hill. They are talking. It is Joe but it is also Artie. She asks him if he killed Artie. He says no. His eyes fly up, look away, like Artie used to do when he lied, so she knew he was lying. So she said again, did you kill Arthur? He said stop asking me that. If someone dies under your care it doesn't mean you killed him. She objects to the phrase "under your care" and she gives him a little push down the hill. Off a cliff. Then she goes back to somewhere and makes salami on thin-sliced rye with mustard and relish the way Artie liked it. The bread curls away from the meat while she waits for him but he never comes back and she puts on the poncho to go out and look for him but falls asleep. Then she is in her car, driving back to the city alone, weaving in and out of traffic like a cowboy on the Taconic. When she gets home, she sees Emily talking to Fred and when Emily asks where Joe is, Sally says, "I dropped him off."

He woke her, at her front door.

You're in one place, then you're in another. She thought of telling him she could not see him again, but instead she told him she could not see him tomorrow. Tomorrow she was seeing Fran.

"I'm sorry I slept through the ride," she said. "I dropped right off."

"I take it as a compliment," he said. "You trust my driving."

What a positive man! was the proper thought, but when she said it, it came out wrong, like a disparagement.

"You're angry at me?" Joe said.

"No. Bad dream."

He started his car and then leaned out the window and hesitated, as though he wanted to say something. And she wanted to say something and ask something amid a surge of such desire for him that it made her stomach ache – but she didn't, and he didn't, and then he waved and drove off.

* * *

Avoidance is an art... There have always been things Sally thought about doing and knew she had to do but did not do. This constituted a specific activity which she thought of as not-doing. She stood at the window, looking out, in a pleasant reverie, at the street of small houses, watched the neighbors for an hour, all the time on her way to cleaning out a closet or looking for a lost glove. The closet might get done another day; the glove might not get found. It was not accidental, either way. The thinking about it, the not-doing it while thinking about it was a balance, which eventually tipped one way or another. She knew this. Through the years she knew without knowing that she was going to buy a new pair of gloves eventually, or that she was going to give up on ever finding the huge silver ring with the amber stone which slipped off her finger one day, or she had let slip off, not-sizing it months after she lost enough weight for her fingers to let the ring go. She knew there had always been something about the ring she didn't like and since it was a gift, couldn't say. So this kind of negligence set in, instead, making her not-size it.

What puzzled her was that sometimes, lately, she did this (not-doing) with things she yearned for, too. Like playing the piano. There, at the window, watching Fred and some woman, she was thinking of Bach Inventions, the sprightly precision, the lovely action of her old Baldwin spinet, ahhh... and right then some aversion reaction set in, and she stayed at the window, instead of going straight to the piano, as she pictured herself going straight to the piano. It had spread to playing recorded music. She might be cooking and suddenly in the silent kitchen she thought, oh, I'd love to hear some Sinatra right now, and then kept on cooking, sometimes acting as though it was a delay based on kitchen efficiency, that she would get to it when she finished beating eggs or chopping onions, sometimes just letting the reverie spin out and replace the actuality of it. The music was not Sinatra, it was the reverie. She hadn't played her CDs in more than a year.

And now, calling Joe Messinger had become like that. Every morning she woke up thinking of him. With her stomach churning, she said into the bathroom mirror, "I have to call Joe today," and then she wandered through her day, putting it off, forgetting it, remembering it with something like a low-grade electric shock to her stomach, which sometimes spread to her fingertips, saying again, "Oh, I must remember to call Joe," before letting it fall back. As if she could forget. And he called and left messages all over the place. She stood there and listened as the message spun out live, loving the sound of his voice, then replaying it out of the machine. "Oh, I must pick up the next time he calls," she said to herself.

The simplest answer was that she did not want to talk with him. Yet in the middle of the night, she woke, remembering his hands on her, the sweetness of his kiss. Hungry for more, she remembered she wanted to see him again. And since you never know what could happen, there really was no time to waste. She said this to herself, too.

* * *

The owner of the red car might have just gone out of town for a long weekend, and had come back to work directly from the airport on the morning of September 11, and had planned that night to pick up his car on Maiden Lane, and pay whatever parking tickets had accrued. Maybe he had parked outside Sally's shop because he liked it. Maybe he said to the car (as Sally talked to hers, sometimes) *wait for me here, in front of this nice and safe and friendly little shop while I'm out of town. I'll come back for you.* But he had never picked up the car. Where had he worked? At the company who lost so many of their employees? At the Stock Exchange? Not even in the building, but his boss had decided to give him a welcome back breakfast at Windows on the World?

* * *

Sally called Joe.

"I knew it was you," he said.

"Don't ask me why I haven't called," she said.

"All right." He waited. "Any other rules?"

She could hear him smiling.

97

"None I can think of now," she said.

"I'm going upstate this weekend. To meet Evan. He's coming down from Albany. Come with me. I'll pick you up Friday at 4."

She remembered the purpose of her call was to tell him she was not going to see him anymore. "Make it 4:30," she said.

* * *

She told him about Emily and Fred. "Am I being... what am I being? Why am I so upset about it? What is it I..."

"You're not being anything," he said. He said it was just another example of the lawlessness of love.

"The lawlessness of love? What a phrase," she said.

He put his arm around her shoulders and gave her a little shake.

"Yes, and try to remember, you're not the sheriff."

They were waiting at the restaurant, a small, cozy stone house in the woods, with a roaring fire. It was a chilly March night. Evan had called to say he'd be late. His wife had an emergency.

"What kind of emergency does a dermatologist have?" Sally said.

Joe wiggled his eyebrows, as if he doubted there was one.

They sipped their drinks and waited, and Sally finally had to ask, what had he thought when she didn't call.

"I thought you were sorry we had slept together," he said. "You want to go back to being a virgin."

She said it was more complicated, but when he asked her in what way, she could not think of any.

"Just so you know, you're not," he said.

"Not a virgin?" she said.

He nodded. "You can't undo what's done, or unsay what's said. That's the rule."

"I don't want to change the rule. I just have a feeling that I'm out of control. That I'm conducting myself... I don't exactly know if I want or don't want this... things seem out of order. Disorderly."

"Disorderly conduct?"

"Not in those words," she said.

"Your words," he said.

All the while he was saying this, scolding her, she thought, he was holding her hand, playing with her fingers, looking into her eyes, making her think of the two of them, leaning against a tree, kissing, of later, in bed.

His son, Evan, it appeared, was standing some distance away, waiting until they stopped talking. They both faced him as he came forward, his face flushed. Had they been speaking loudly? Had he heard?

"Wendy couldn't make it," he said, and in the way he averted his eyes when he said it, Sally could see that something might not be right between Evan and Wendy.

"That's okay," Joe said quickly, and stood up, pulling his son into a hug. It was such sweet, unconditional support that it brought tears to her eyes. I would be too busy sussing out the blame, she thought. He introduced them, putting a hand on her shoulder, as if he wanted to link them all.

Dinner was subdued, despite everyone's effort. Finally, Joe followed his son's lead and talked about neutral things and medical things and Sally let her attention wander to the table next to theirs. The people were talking about their kids, who were about to buy a house that had rooms that were so small they could not fit night tables next to their bed, and were thinking of removing a fireplace in the bedroom to make more space. Sally had an opinion, which was to keep the fireplace because it would add resale value. When they turned and stared at her, she realized she had said it out loud. She laughed and pointed at her wineglass, as if she had one too many, and said "sorry," and they laughed and one person commented that she had made a good point. Joe and Evan did not comment, though she thought she saw Evan's eyes touch the scene and draw back.

Back at the house, Sally left father and son alone to talk. She went to the smaller spare bedroom, and turned on the late news, and by the time Joe came in, she was dozing. She felt his kiss, but she didn't stir, and after a moment, he turned off the television and tiptoed out.

Next morning when she woke, both bedroom doors were closed, so she prepared coffee and went about preparing breakfast, setting the table with cold cereal, strawberries, bagels they had brought from Bagel Oasis in Queens. She was aware she was creating this domestic tableau for Joe's son, to make a good impression, even though she told herself she didn't care.

The country morning was perfect, like one of those run-of-the-mill, cut-rate greeting cards, a little too picturesque for Sally's taste: morning dew sparkling just right on the light green spring grass, like silica dust on the front of cheap cardstock. How about a little action here, she thought, as a family of deer sauntered across the lawn. The big one, the father, she thought, seemed to sense her at the window and lifted his face and focused big, sleepy-looking eyes on her, then turned his back and lifted his white tail, showing her his asshole, which broke the perfection, and she laughed. "Back at you," she said.

She heard the gravel crunch outside and the downstairs door opened and Joe and Evan came in, all ruddy from a walk.

"I thought you guys were sleeping. Here I was tiptoeing around," she said.

"We didn't want to wake you," Evan said, looking concerned, as if he might have offended her, and she thought, *who wound you up so tight?*

"No, that's fine," she said. "I'm not much of a walker, anyway. Ready for coffee?"

During breakfast, the conversation turned to housing and school systems, from which Sally intuited either that Evan's wife was pregnant or they were thinking about it. Afterward, as he was about to go, Joe asked him if it was all right to tell Sally the news.

"How wonderful," she said, as if she had not figured it out already. She reached out to give him a hug, but he stepped back, holding his hand out stiffly, so she shook it.

"It's good," he said, nodding, tight-jaw, tight smile.

After he left, she asked Joe. "Was that me, or is he not exactly happy about it?"

"She's got a family history," he said. "Tay Sachs. And with everything else..."

"What else?"

He rubbed his eyes and said he didn't want to talk about it right now. Sally nodded. "But sometime?" she said, and he said yes.

"Tay Sachs is nothing to sneeze at. She must be frightened."

"They both are," he said.

She wanted to ask him then the question that was in her mind. Or something close to it. She could just say, "Do you ever see such suffering that you want to put an end to it?" without being specific.

But certain thoughts might be better left un-thought, and if you can't manage to do that, if you thought them anyway, better left unsaid. She pressed her lips together so she would be sure not to blurt it out. But Joe turned to her with such a look on his face, that she wondered if she had done it anyway.

* * *

Sally went for a check-up; the wait in the doctor's office was very long. Sometimes, Sally calmed down when she waited, and sometimes she got so nervous that when the nurse took her blood pressure it had gone up and she had to explain herself, making a joke about white coat hypertension, using the phrase confidently, as if it did not embarrass her. But this day she was calm. The doctor came into the room and said she was "very pleased" with Sally's vitals. "You must be doing something right," she said. So now she and the doctor traded pleasantries, and then got down to business. Anything in particular bothering her, the doctor asked, getting ready to move on to the next examining room, a needier patient. And as if it were a small matter, Sally said, "Actually I have some concern. I have been getting a bit forgetful."

"That's not uncommon, at your age," the doctor said, reassuringly. "Not even at mine," she said. This was meant to be funny and self-deprecating, Sally knew. The doctor was barely fifty.

"Well, it's a little more than that, actually," Sally said. "I find that I'm blurting things out, things I'm thinking but don't mean to say. And I laugh and cry easily. Maybe... almost... involuntarily. And my temper is flaring up at little things."

"Ever since 9/11, you would be surprised how much of that I am hearing," the doctor said.

But Sally noticed she had stopped writing and was paying attention, and her stomach tightened, because as much as she wanted to be taken seriously, she hoped she wouldn't be. She continued. "And I'm not sleeping, and I've become obsessed..." She had been about to say *with this man who asks me to get naked in daylight, who thinks everything is wonderful all the time, including me,* but switched it to, "By a red car which was parked outside my office on 9/11 and was unclaimed, or, I mean I don't know if it was unclaimed, because now it's gone, but I can't seem to get it out of my mind."

The doctor shrugged as if she granted it was a bit much, but was still not ready to be alarmed. "Are you depressed?"

"I never cared for the word," Sally said. "It's a self-indulgent word. Let's say some days I'm sad, some days I'm not." What she doesn't say is, *some days I am a maniac, happier than I've ever been, and I've embarked on this venture, this adventure, and it would*

be a most inopportune time to lose my brain. What she didn't say is
*I'm falling in love and I don't know whether it is because I am losing
my brain or not.*

The doctor raised her eyebrows and obviously took that as
a yes, because she said she would be glad to write a script for
something mild. Zoloft. 25 milligrams and see how she does.
Sally declined.

"Well, if it persists, we'll look into it some more," the doctor
said.

"My mother had Alzheimer's," Sally said. "Or anyway,
vascular dementia."

The doctor typed it into her chart. "Well, as I say, if it persists,"
she said. "Sally," Dr. Carlino said. "Who is the President?"

"Bush," she said. "The son."

"And what is today?"

"Thursday," she said.

"No, what is the date?" Dr. Carlino said.

"Oh, I don't know, April ninth, is it?"

"It is," the doctor said, satisfied. "And the year?"

"Eighteen sixty-nine," Sally said, and for a moment the doctor
didn't see that she was joking, but then she did and smiled.

"Oh, you're fine, I really think you are," she said. "Take the
Zoloft and see how you do. Break the pill in half. And I promise,
if this persists, we will look into it further. But at this point, I
don't know that you want to start with CAT scans and MRIs and
all sorts of diagnostics. There just doesn't seem to be a reason.
Be glad, Sally."

On the way out of the doctor's office, suddenly Sally
remembered again how urgently she desired to know if the
owner of the red car had ever come back and claimed it. Or
if they had carted it away. She thought about it all week. And
she did not want to remind CJ to ask her journalist friend to
track down the license plate number, which Sally told her and
then put away, for safekeeping, someplace. But its whereabouts

had eluded her all week, until this moment, when all at once she remembered, and hurried home, rummaging briefly in the small plastic container at the top of her closet, and under drugstore envelopes of miscellaneous photos she had never had time to catalog, for a small silver evening bag on a tarnished silver chain. Upon finding the box she retrieved its lovely French name: *minaudiere* – and there, amidst old keys to jewelry boxes, treasure chests long ago discarded, the formula for a shade of blonde hair dye left to her by her last hairdresser who had retired to Florida, and a single earring of a pair which once belonged to Susie, was the slip of paper with the license plate number of the red car. The paper itself has a fine grit on its surface. Once she saw it there, safe, ready to be used, she felt the urgency slip away and she put it back, picking up, instead, the earring, thinking she would put it on a chain, make it a necklace, but finally, putting it, too, back in the box. She went back to the photos, and took out one envelope – she knew exactly which one it was – of pictures which she has not wanted to paste into her book, could not have, really, but did not want to discard.

Sally had always been a reluctant photographer. Since she was partial to words, she didn't like pictures that rendered the words valueless. Why struggle over the description of a sunset when some insipid postcard did you one better? So she could have skipped the camera. And though Artie had had little interest in actually *taking* pictures, he thought it was the right thing to do, because families had family albums. He was always asking, *Did you buy film? Did you forget the camera?* before boarding a plane to wherever they were going. But then he always lost interest and left the actual picture-taking to her. Sometimes, in a warm climate, when she was lazy with the sun and uninterested in documenting another seaside or lakeside, she had given in to the ease of the camera. When the children were small, she memorialized birthdays, Thanksgivings, school plays and pageants. It was her secret that she did it precisely because she had so little interest in those occasions that it seemed all right to leave them to a camera. If it had been up to her, she might have designed a greeting card that said, *Is there anything duller than a sixth-grade dance recital?*

The photos she held out now were from those early days: black and white, with that old-fashioned deckled edge that photos used to have. Sally remembered the day: another backyard party, this one for Fran's eighth birthday, and Emily was two and in the midst of being toilet trained, and was held up in the arms of one of the many guests who had passed her around that day, appreciating her bubbly personality despite a full, stinky diaper, as this photo reified: the child's happiness mid-laugh, the adult's olfactory discomfort mid-smell, hand under the ripe, full diaper bottom. It was the kind of photo that would have been a great greeting card with the right caption. She couldn't think of one at the moment. Then there were the rest of them, from that day. She slid them out, turned them on their faces, like they were Tarot cards, to be read. She turned one. A slight woman with a helmet of hair which looked sepia but which Sally knew was what they used to call "dirty blonde." Caught around the waist by a man's arms, she was bending backward, her mouth grotesque in mid-laugh. She had been that way since the day Sally snapped the picture, some thirty odd years ago, mid-laugh, out of breath. Out of life now, Sally thought. The man was Artie and the woman was her late friend, Ann. She remembered the day, the backyard party. Innocent horsing around. Turned the next picture. The exhale of the big laugh, the reversal, the forward bend, this time Ann's head against Artie's polo shirt. You could notice her hair split down the back, as if it had not been washed lately. She turned another picture. This one showed no one's face. One face against the other face obliterating the view of either. Around the side of the house, near the rose bush which did so poorly for so many years until lightning struck the tree which blocked its sun and

105

the tree died and now the rose bush is flourishing, the spot where the two were standing half covered by errant branches. Next picture, dim in the shadows cast by the setting sun, after everyone else had gone in, and the briquets were cooling. You see the two bodies, Ann's arms were up, under Artie's armpits, he was so much taller than she, Arthur's arms looped downward, around her waist. Sally and Artie were almost the same height so he never reached down like that to embrace her. She thought now, there was something very nurturing about his hold on Ann. She had framed and focused the shot and just sat there, at the upstairs window, not snapping, struck by how tender the downward hold was, and of course she contemplated not snapping it, or rather, snapping it into her memory only and leaving the film blank, but then her finger had decided for her and there it was. And here it is.

She saved the baby Emily photo, and ripped the rest of them in half, quarters, eighths, and kept ripping until they were confetti which she took downstairs and sprinkled into the garbage and covered with grinds from the morning coffee.

And she thought she had put the memory to rest. And now, for the time being or maybe forever, she was also going to put the red car out of her mind.

* * *

In early April, something was off in her bedroom. She noticed it when she came home from the weekend away, and again when she came back from her doctor's appointment. She looked around carefully, missing something but not knowing what. Then, she saw that the small picture over the night table on Artie's side of the bed, "The Daffodils," was gone. She looked behind the table itself, to see if it had fallen off or slid down, but it was not there. "Well, never mind," she said.

But it continued to bother her. A picture can't just disappear, can it? She decided to ask Alicia, the cleaning woman, when she comes on Friday.

Alicia said it had been gone for a while, and she thought Sally had taken it down. "Put away," is what she said Sally did.

"Why would I do that?" she asked Alicia, "Why?"

Alicia didn't know, but why would she?

"Why would she? Why would Alicia take your daffodil picture and not tell you?" Fran said.

"I don't know. Maybe she broke the frame or the glass and she didn't want to say."

"Mom, please. She's been working here for twenty-two years. She's broken Waterford crystal and hasn't lied about it."

"Well, I don't know," Sally said, impatiently. "But it's gone and I don't know."

It led her to a habit of waking every morning and taking inventory. Clock, rocker, mirror, pictures. One day her diamond ring was missing. The ring she never took off.

"Except for washing, sleeping and cooking," Fran said.

"I checked every pocket of every apron and robe. Blouse pockets. Jackets." Because when her fingers swelled she sometimes did take her rings off. She checked the drawer of the night table. She asked Alicia if she had seen it, and got a strange look.

"No, I don't think she took it," she told Fran. "But I had to ask. I rather think that the man who cleaned the radiators last year made a copy of my key and came in here while I was away and found it on the night table and took it."

"Are you kidding?" Fran said.

"I know it sounds crazy," Sally said. "But I just wonder. I did not like the looks of him."

Then she found it on the sink shelf.

Alicia gave notice.

And now, the children have invited themselves for dinner. What in the name of heaven was going on? Was Emily going to marry Fred and adopt Marcie? Had Fran done some violence to Dan? Mark... well, Mark was gunning for her, she knew that. But of course she knew it was not any of those things. She strongly suspected it was – what did they call it nowadays? – an intervention. Something about her and Joe? Or about the daffodil picture business? Or the silly business of her ring? After which Alicia quit?

They were all outside on the patio, the girls, Mark and Fred, Rita, who had invited herself last minute.

"Oh, Fred, how nice," she said. "I didn't know you were coming."

"Mom?" Emily said.

"I said 'how nice' Emily," Sally said.

"Doug's here, Mom," Fran said. To change the subject? Are they handling her?

"Well where is he?" Sally said, looking behind her chair, as if she might have missed a seventeen-year-old grandson somewhere on the patio.

"He's walking the dog," Fran said. "I bought him a dog."

"Well, THAT's news," Sally said.

"Is he spayed?" Rita asked.

"Yes, Aunt Ree," Fran said. "But with a dog it's called 'neutered.'"

"Well, I don't know what it's called," Rita said. "It's when they cut off the dog's Turks and Caicos."

Fran hesitated, but then just said, "Yes."

The children always wanted dogs, but they had never gotten one and Sally believed that they held it against her.

"I would never let you have one," Sally said.

"I know," Emily said. "Why was that? You always seemed to like them when they belonged to someone else."

She didn't think about her answer, she just said it, like it was something she had always known. "Because they are sexual predators."

Everyone stopped talking. Sally was a little taken aback when it came out of her mouth, but she had to laugh at the looks on their faces. She did not mean to say it, or had gotten the words a little wrong, but it was said, so what was the big deal?

"Don't be so shocked," she said. "I don't mean really *predators*, but they are awfully interested in crotches, sometimes, and it used to make me nervous."

"Mom!" Fran said.

"What, Fran. I just mean the way they sniff around. My aunt had a Doberman, once, Skipper, and he used to come up and put his big snout against me, you-know-where. And I remember thinking, next time I am not going to back up, I am going to stand there and let him, and see what he wants. I didn't ever do it, but I remember thinking it."

"Mom, please!" Fran said again.

"Disinhibition," Emily said, darkly.

Mark looked like he was going to pass out.

"Well, you asked why I would never have one and I told you."

Maybe it was a dirty thought, but she would not erase any thoughts anymore, no matter how dirty, no matter how mean. If she was being erased already, if her brain was being erased, she would not hurry the process by even one word or one thought. Such a beautiful story she once read, about a daughter who found evidence of her father's pornographic interests, upon his death and it shook her. William Trevor or Peter Taylor. And the daughter tells her mother and her mother says she always knew.

"Speaking of dogs, there was a dog in the debris, downtown, after 9/11," she said. "I read it somewhere." The papers made a fuss about it. She guessed it was easier to make a fuss about a dog. The dog belonged to the man who owned the magazine kiosk, who survived because he was out sick that day. His son-in-law had taken over the stand, and he and the dog were killed.

Still no one spoke.

"Well," she said. "Let's change the subject." And when no one said anything then, she changed it herself. "I am suddenly disgusted by the sound of operatic tenors. I can't explain it and I don't want to. They make me physically nauseous. That big-chested, rib-opening sound, which I used to love, no. The other day I heard someone singing like that and I wanted to vomit," she said. It is a mildly interesting thought that she had not planned to share, but why not?

Fran said, "Oh. My. God."

Mark got up and went into the house.

"Bring the glasses and the wine," Sally called after him. "I left them on the counter," thinking what were they going to do, wash her mouth out with soap?

* * *

There is a lot at stake when you shift your allegiance. When you fall in love. You keep things from your already-loved ones that you and your newly-loved one absolutely need to share alone. And it is not only what you keep deliberately, but other things, too, that fall by the wayside. In fact, you are trading what you get – new love with the secret or disapproved-of one (wrong gender, wrong person, whatever else it is that's objectionable) with what you already have – family love, ease, routine, life-as-you-know-it. And eventually it is not only felt by you. All the others in your up-to-now life sense what has been withdrawn from them: they are no longer welcome to pop in on you, they don't get your free time and attention, old routines are gone, your unchallenged interest in their lives has been replaced by a consuming interest in the new love. Its makeshift structure, before you know if it will stand forever, is intricate and bolstered by unending attention. It is a make-believe version of an altered life.

Sally knew this. Or, rather, she lived it with slight awareness. There was no longer time for long talks with CJ; no interest in the bizarre configurations of love in Emily's life, or their lack in Fran's. If Mark wanted to unmarry or remarry Robin, it was all right with Sally. She could suddenly even talk politics with her son. Constant granny was disappearing, and this worried the children. They called each other with stories about what was missing from their lives, the quotes and quips and fixes and frames, all of which she had provided for them. And also a new carelessness about what they thought: they saw it and they didn't like it. And the disinhibition, especially, the psychologist's insider phrase Emily had taught them all, that they have all adopted. She was so blunt and physically out there. They gathered together to complain. They thought they were losing her, or more specifically, that she was losing IT. They wanted to intercept her, take care of her, advise her, stop her in her tracks and cut her off at the pass, from wherever it was she thought she was going. But this night, instead, she served them a beautiful sausage and peppers dinner, got all the seasonings right, and told them to go to hell, if not in so many words. And at the same time, convinced them once and for all she was going to the dogs.

* * *

Being a psychologist, Emily knew body language. And since she didn't want to betray the fact that she didn't like Joe, and did not want to appear hostile, she was careful not to cross her arms in front of her chest. She kept them folded in her lap. She noticed *he* was holding on to the arms of his leather desk chair, tightly.

"I guess you're wondering why I'm here," she said.

"I'm sure it's about your mother," he said. "Your mother and me?"

Emily shook her head. "My mother's a big girl," she said. "And my father's been gone a long time."

He didn't say anything, so Emily had to say, "Then why am I here?" and he nodded. She took a deep breath. "This is difficult," she said.

He let go of the arms of the chair then. That was his territory, handling difficult stuff. He is an oncologist, after all. It may have been a long time ago, when he was taking care of her father, but she shivered at the thought that her father sat in that seat, or her mother, and had their bad news handled... handed to them by Joe.

"We are concerned about my mother. Worried about her. She's not herself. She is showing some signs of... change."

"I know," he said.

This surprised Emily. She wanted to ask him how he knew, or what he knew, but she was afraid. It was hard enough to hold onto what she and her siblings thought they knew, or feared they knew. It was hard to speak about. "We think she may be having some... brain problems." She snorted. "That sounds stupid, but it's hard to verbalize. All right. Little strokes? TIAs? Or God forbid, Alzheimer's. She's distracted. She's forgetful. But it's more than that. She's... not herself. She's... I don't know, unbuttoned, you know? I know that's frontal lobe. She blurts things out. She's blunt and vulgar..." Here she stopped, as it occurred to her that some of what she was saying sounded as if she might be blaming it on Joe's influence. Maybe it was Joe's influence. She sighed. "My mother was never vulgar."

"I know," he said. "Your mother is not vulgar," he said.

Emily's hands were like ice, and body language or not, her knuckles were white. "What do you mean you know?"

"Your mother is aware she is getting a little forgetful and she is looking into it."

She had so many questions: What did he mean looking into it? How long had this been going on? "Why didn't she say anything to me?" she said.

He raised his eyebrows, but did not say that Emily has been busy with her own life, that they all are, which made her think it.

"I know this sounds defensive, but do you know," Emily said, "that she sent Freddy a picture of him holding me when I was a baby in diapers with a note insinuating he was a pervert?" Freddy had showed it to her. At first, she had laughed. But Freddy didn't think it was funny, and they had almost had their first fight because of it. "It's not funny," she said, because now Joe was smiling.

He shrugged. "It's not that serious," he said, "and you have to admit even if it isn't perverted it *is* a little perverse, in an amusing way. Don't you think, Emily? But I don't think it's for you and me to talk about. Talk to your mother."

It galled her that he was right. "What the hell do you want from her?" she blurted. "Now?" She had tried to be tactful, cagey, work up to asking for his advice, what he suggested, what steps she and her sister and brother should take. "I'm sorry," she said. "But if you know my mother is going this way..." What was in her mind? What absurdity was she thinking? How he would take advantage of her? "Well, this just doesn't seem the time to start a relationship."

He spread his hands on the top of his desk, wide open, as if he had nothing hidden in them. Nothing up his sleeve, either. "Who knows when the right time is. Your mother says there is always cholera somewhere."

"But if she's not *herself?*" Emily insisted.

He shrugged. "I never said she isn't herself," he said. "And anyway, I like whoever she is," he said. "I love whoever she is." His cheeks reddened. And then he turned his hands over and used them to push himself up, and he came around the desk and lifted her by her arm and walked her to the door. And when he got her to the door, he said very quietly, "And that's all

I am going to explain to you," before he gave her a gentle push across the threshold and closed his office door behind her.

* * *

When Sally first heard about the shoe bomber, caught on a plane from Paris to Miami, she thought it was a joke, some inept wannabe terrorist's idea of the next thing, something dreamed up by Maxwell Smart and agent 99. But at the airport, watching travelers take their shoes off brought tears to her eyes.

"Why cry?" Joe asked.

She had driven him to Kennedy, for his flight to Los Angeles.

"For what used to be. For how carefree we were and we didn't even know enough to value it."

Artie would have said, "Put it out of your mind. That was then, this is now."

But Sally always wondered how things and people got from then to now, and here to there, from meaning to be a good boy and ending up a bad boy, a felon, a shoe bomber. "That's a fact," Joe said. "You can't help thinking that six months ago if someone told you you would have to remove your shoes to make sure you weren't carrying a bomb, you would have laughed. And now you cry."

They had this conversation as they were lingering outside the security area, and the line to go through to the gate was getting longer and longer and she noticed that though he was still talking to her, he was ready to go, one foot facing the people lining up, the leg bouncing impatiently, taking an occasional glance toward the Hudson News kiosk just beyond where people were retrieving their belongings that the moving scanner belt had disgorged.

"I wish you were coming," he said. And at the moment, ready to see him go away for a week, she wished it too. But earlier in the week, she heard him planning and thought how glad she was she had said no. She had done her ride-alongs, as she called them, when Artie had gone to conventions in Spain, and London, and Chicago and San Diego, and she had gone along, being the wife half the time, and resisting it the rest of the time, alienating the wives with her not-so-subtle references to her business, how hard it had been to get away for five days, how no, she couldn't go shopping with the girls, she had to go upstairs and call her assistant, or an important client. Now, probably most of the wives were working women, but not then.

"Well, you'll be home before you know it," she said.

And she kissed him goodbye and told him to be safe. He said he would, and she should try not to worry about shoe bombers and bad boys.

The minute he left, the family descended on her.

It turned out that Fran had bought the dog for Douglas because he was suffering, shaken by the divorce, seeing his father move out, and even more, Sally suspected, finding himself one-on-one with his fierce mother, while his brother was safely away at college. What was worse: Fran's scathing attention, or the long hours spent alone in the house while the rest of the family was out doing things? Neither was good, and Douglas acted out in the usual ways: sinking grades, skipping school, occasional risky mouthing off to his teachers – he wouldn't dare with his mother – and a sudden interest in wearing all black. This last, funnily enough, disturbed Fran most. She saw on the evening news that every unhappy little monster who ended up shooting up a school, was dressed in black. She called it "garth" and raked her fingers through her hair in despair, and got him a dog. Douglas named him Dobby, after the elf in Harry Potter, and the first week they had him, Douglas got into a fight with someone at the dog park who called Dobby stupid, and was expelled for hitting the name caller. Sweet Douglas, who used to carry ants out of the house in his palm rather than crush them, was now being accused of violence. He must have surprised himself most of all, Sally said, when she heard the story. The name caller threatened to file charges against Douglas, except that he had hit back and given Douglas a black eye. Now, Douglas didn't want to leave the house, even to walk the dog. This was where Sally came in, when Fran told her. Up till now, she had been in the dark about the sudden upheaval in her youngest grandchild's life. "Why didn't you tell me? What are you doing?"

"I'm trying to keep it in perspective," Fran said.

"Well, maybe you shouldn't," Sally said, impatiently. "Not now. This is an emergency. Something you have to face. Not something to minimize so you can go on writing airtight insurance contracts."

Fran was floored.

"Fran, Doug is in trouble," Sally said. "Look at him. Face it. He's been depressed for a long time. And you've got to do something NOW, not leave it to a dog to fix. A dog is all well and good, but the boy needs his mother. And his father." Fran had been using this keep-it-in-perspective bullshit as her get-out-of-jail-free card. So she could bypass action. She could postpone, delay, pretend everything was all right. To keep that goddamn game face, to mask her rage or grief, to use the long view to sit on her ass and do nothing. How was it Sally had never thought this before? How could she not have noticed it? Is this what she did, too?

And while Fran was mulling it over, CJ showed up at Sally's door on Thursday. "What a surprise!" Sally said, meaning what's wrong?

CJ began to cry. Sally let her cry until she ran out of tears, thinking how easy it was to know which tears were grief and which tears were drama and which tears were self-pity and which tears were buying time.

"Do your parents know you're here?" she said.

They were sitting on the sofa in the sunroom, and Sally had

spread the afghan over both their knees. She smoothed CJ's hair back, let it fall forward, smoothed it back, playing for time, herself, waiting for her granddaughter to speak.

CJ said no, they didn't know she was here.

"We're going to have to tell them, CJ," Sally said. "I'm not having your father accuse me of kidnapping."

Her granddaughter smiled weakly, not yet ready to give up the role of tragic heroine. She was wearing jeans and a bulky sweater and a down vest, and she looked radiantly sad, with her cheeks flushed from crying, and tears shimmering brightly on her eyelids. Sally hugged her hard. "All right, we'll wait until you get it off your chest. But if you don't want to call, you'd better talk, now, baby. Your choice. Are you pregnant?"

CJ looked shocked. "No!"

"Have you had an abortion? Are you on drugs? Did you rob a bank? Get caught cheating on an exam? Kill someone? Drive a car into a tree? Get bitten by a rabid squirrel? Owe someone money? Have you been gambling?"

"Grandma, stop," the girl said.

"I just want you to know, whatever it is, it can be fixed. It is not what happens to you in life, it is what you do about what happens."

And something did happen: the saying suddenly sounded canned and stupid in Sally's own ears. She heard it the way CJ herself might be hearing it: silly, smelling slightly of mothballs, part of grandma's same-old, same-old. She was tired of it herself. Tired of herself, and tired of sayings. Even tired of this favorite grandchild. She was tired. Her eyes began to leak.

This frightened CJ so much that she broke open and spilled it all.

"I'm in love with someone and it's no good," CJ said, miserably.

Sally sighed. She was relieved, though she knew how much pain young love could bring. Now it was only a matter of waiting for the details. The rest would come.

"Someone older," Sally guessed. "Your journalist?"

"Who's also my English professor," CJ said.

"And married, I suppose."

CJ nodded.

"And does he love you?" Sally said.

"Yes," CJ said. "She does."

Sally almost didn't get it; and then she did.

Sally's daughter-in-law, Robin, called in the morning. "I think it's about a boy," she said.

"Sounds that way," Sally said, because she'd be damned if she was going to give her any advanced notice. She would wait and talk with Mark. "At least it isn't anorexia," Sally said. "She's eating fine." But Robin was not so easily distracted.

"I know, but I'm worried," she said. "She's under such emotional pressure, what with the divorce and everything... I just want her to be okay." And her voice trembled. Sally almost gave in. "I think it's about a boy," Robin repeated. "Or a girl."

What? What did she say? "Are you saying CJ is a lesbian?" Sally said. Daring her. Thinking how dare she? Thinking how did she know?

"I'm just giving an example," Robin said.

"Well, it's an example about a lesbian," Sally said.

"It's a new day, Sally," she said. "It happens." And she hung up before Sally could think of what to answer.

Mark showed up in the afternoon.

"You should have waited," Sally said.

"She's my daughter," he said. "She should come home, to her parents, not to her grandmother."

"Mark, it's not a contest," she said.

"She's my daughter," he said. "I have a right."

What right? To make a scene? To make a mess? Suddenly Sally was mad, mad. "Why are you so aggrieved? What the hell are you so aggrieved about all the time? You have two wonderful children and you don't appreciate either one of them, you made Robbie so competitive he won't even compete anymore, and CJ."

The way to Mark's heart is through his ears. Shout loud enough and he'll listen, he'll even back down.

"All right, all right," he said. "But I'm worried. "CJ..." – he called through the closed door – "Are you all right?"

Sally heard her mumbling on the other side and suddenly thought Mark was right. This is their dance. Let me leave them to dance it. And she retreated to the kitchen. She felt heat and saw that she had left the stove on again. This was the third time. Number three senior moment.

* * *

So Sally talked to things. Her car. The nice hot water in the shower. "You're beautiful," she said to the showerhead. "You've got just the right pressure, like you know who is under you."

She hadn't heard CJ come in to brush her teeth. "Grandma?" she said.

"Talking to the showerhead," Sally said. And suddenly wondered if that was all right. Or if it was a sign of something really terrible. Or, if CJ would think it was a sign of something really terrible, and would that be better or worse than if it actually was a sign?

"Don't worry, I'm not losing it. What are you going to do?" she asked, partially to deflect her from the shower-talk.

"I don't know," CJ said.

"I just want to say before you make a decision to become a lesbian, that it is still a very uncomfortable lifestyle." She had been thinking about it, talking to Showerhead, and they had decided, since this was CJ's English teacher, that the class had just read *The Yellow Wallpaper* or some other seminal work, which had influenced the child. Showerhead warned Sally not

119

to say so.

"I'm not making any decisions like that," CJ said. "But what if that's what I am? Mom and Dad want me to go back to Doctor Feldheim. Is that the first thing everyone thinks when you tell them you are in love if they don't happen to approve of who you're in love with? Send me to a shrink? I mean fifty years ago they would have put me in an insane asylum."

"Listen darling, this is your decision. You may love this professor of yours, or maybe you have mistranslated your admiration into sexual terms, because in some way that's easier. Maybe she led you on. Maybe you really want a mother figure. Think it through. Wait till the end of your semester, at least. Wait till you get your grade."

That was a low blow, Sally knew. But suddenly and again, the antic nature of the whole enterprise hit her, and she really didn't want to take it seriously anymore.

"What is it you want to happen now that you've told us? Are you running away together? Are you Coming Out? Are you dropping out? Or are you just after making your parents pay? Pass me the towel."

Sally stepped out of the shower, and CJ, who was sitting on the closed toilet seat, looked a little shocked. Sally had never spoken to her this way before. "Is your girlfriend leaving her family and running away with you?"

"No," she said, sullenly.

"Then what's the point of all this? Besides making yourself and everyone who knows you very, very upset? And turn off the waterworks. Crying stops you from thinking. What does your beloved say?"

"She said she doesn't want to see me anymore."

"Okay. Sounds like a plan. Now, back to my question. What are you going to do?"

She was still sniffling.

"Go into the bedroom and sit down with a pad and paper

and write down all your choices. Then come back and we'll have lunch and review them."

When Sally peeked into the bedroom an hour later, CJ was packing. Going back to school. She had a paper due at the end of the week, she said. Her eyes were red but she wasn't crying.

Before she left, she hugged Sally and said, "She smokes. I can't stand the smell."

"Now that's something wonderful," said Sally.

* * *

On the way to the airport to get Joe, Sally made a wrong turn on a street she had turned on scores of times, and that got her confused, so that by the time she righted herself, she was twenty minutes late and drenched with terror sweat, made worse by his obvious relief. "I didn't know if you were coming," he said.

"Why wouldn't I?" she snapped, but then admitted what happened. (As easily as if she has not spent a lifetime keeping her shortcomings secret.) "I got lost again."

He hugged her. "Well, here you are, so I guess you made it. Not to worry, Sally. You're okay. We all get lost. You were probably distracted. Couldn't wait to see me." He grinned. "Yes? Maybe?"

Well, yes, why could that not be true? She was not losing it; she was distracted and excited to see Joe again. She let the worry drop and felt a small but persuasive gust of happiness in the air around her. And that changed everything. The rush of people in the terminal did not frighten her, for a change.

It was like V-J Day, she thought. Sailors kissing nurses. Children banging pots. No one, no matter how foreign, no matter what they were doing, was a terrorist. The tan man with the black eyes would unwind his turban in the safety of his home, somewhere in Queens, and wrap his wife in it, to show his love. The bulging luggage carried innocent gifts of candy and perfume. Politics was personal.

He hugged her again, hard. "Let's get out of town," he said.

"Oh, yes," she said.

They made a quick stop at her place, to pick up her bag and change cars, and were on the road by early afternoon. By the time they were upstate, her mood had shifted again, and she felt jittery and tearful, angry and happy at the same time. She wanted to shake him. Why did he go away in the first place? Why had she to endure such a stressful homecoming, driving out to JFK, which she hated doing, to get him? How could she have forgotten to pack her robe and slippers? Where were her glasses? Why couldn't she find her goddamn glasses?

She took hold of his shoulders to shake him, but she didn't shake him. She kissed him. She meant to kiss him sincerely, and then get on with the evening, with dinner, with talk of his trip, and her family involvements. But she kissed him hungrily, and they put dinner off until after they had made love.

After sex with Artie, she would lie comfortably and safely in his arms, glad the exertion was over, the snuggling her payoff, and there she would stay, until she or he would say, "Okay?" and turn over to go to sleep. Or one heard the other's snores.

Now, with Joe, she was left with sadness after, the leftover embrace not for comfort and safety, but to hold onto the passion a little longer, and she felt each time that she was counting off, as if it was the tree of present life and she was picking branches, and soon enough it would be bare. "Melancholy," she said.

Joe said that was why it was described as the "little death." "Petit Mort," he said. Medically, some people actually lose consciousness after coitus, he said. But it had come to mean the melancholy, too, the transient nature of the act, the fleeting of orgasmic joy.

Which led her to think speaking of death, what about Arthur? But they hadn't had dinner, and it did not seem the time.

Another time she said it. "What about Arthur?"

And eventually he told her.

"Arthur was in terrible pain," he said.

"I know," she said.

"No, you don't," he said. "Even more than you knew. He didn't want you to know."

"Well, I knew," she said. There was no air in her chest.

"And he asked me..."

"Never mind," she said. "Not now."

When she got back to the city, Emily came by for lunch.

"I had the strangest dream," Emily said. "I dreamed I was talking to you, but you were not only yourself, you were a doctor. And I was telling you that I thought Joe killed Daddy. And you corrected me. You said 'you mean mercy-killed.' And you were right. I did mean mercy-killed."

"I know you kids have thought that," Sally said.

"Well, you did, too," Emily said.

"Yes," Sally said.

When Daddy was so sick at the end. Did Joe... help him to die," Emily said.

"He didn't."

"You asked him?"

"Yes." Though she hadn't.

"Well, what did you expect him to say, Mother? For God's sake."

"You're wrong. He'd tell me."

Which is why she could not bear to ask. And in some other way, she was sure she already knew. But ever since he had told her he had his eye on her when Arthur was his patient, she could not get it out of her mind that in some, subtle way he wanted to get Arthur out of the way so he could have her for himself.

It was stuck in her mind. It was why she had this terrible resistance to seeing him that turned into an exacerbating joy when he came into view. She feared and was thrilled at what he might have done, how he might have rescued her from being the wife of an invalid, and made her a widow. And how awful would the inappropriate, youthful, exuberant joy she felt when he was near, be, if it was paid for by Arthur's death? In bed, she held him against her, and they wrestled and she didn't know if it was the urge to kill him or to climb him that made her breathe so hard.

"What if, in some subtle way, without even knowing it, he wanted to get Dad out of the way so he could have me for himself?"

But Emily pulled back from that. "I'm sure it wasn't that, Mom," she said. With that patronizing tone Sally recognized. Oh, mother is being extreme again.

"How can you be sure?" Sally said. "He noticed me before Daddy was dead."

To which Emily replied, with a glance at her wrist (which was watchless), that she had to run, she had no idea it was that late, she had a client in half an hour.

* * *

How did a person get from Point A to Point B when they were so many miles apart? How did a businessman end up homeless out on the street? How did a prom queen end up ten years later running over and over her prom king husband with the late model Lexus he had just leased for her? How did someone who started out in life as one thing turn into another? Here was an ordinary doctor, someone who did his job well and routinely, day after day after year, having thoughts about a terminal patient's wife, and then, how far from there was it to Point B? To putting the patient to death? How could he NOT have seen how right it was to put Arthur out of his misery and... all right, not to have Sally to himself, because he had not even contacted her for five years, but, but, but, but, but... and what if he had known what was in her mind in those days? Yes, her mind. What if they were already connected as they are now, in some electric, unwavering way? What if he knew that she was thinking she was so tired of seeing Artie die and she was wishing he were dead? What if he had done it for her? How could she bear it?

Seeing him settled her mind. When he was right there, she looked at him and for that moment did not believe he killed Arthur.

* * *

But it didn't stay settled, and so finally she said, "Let's see this through," and he said all right.

"He was in terrible pain," he said, and this time she nodded, so he could continue. "He asked me what I could do. I told him. Opioids. Morphine drip. I asked him if he wanted to try marijuana, but I don't think it would have affected pain for him, at that level, at that time."

"Did he ask you to kill him?"

"He asked me what I thought."

"Don't tiptoe around it, Joe. I want to know."

"Eventually he did. He asked me what I thought. And at first, I told him what the laws were."

"And then...?"

"Arthur was no fool. He asked me if there were ways to get around them, and what they were."

"What were they? What did you tell him?"

"You have to understand, this took place over a long period of time."

"What did you tell him?"

At first, he had told him nothing but tried to dissuade him from opting out in this way. He mentioned the children, his wife. Her. Eventually, when he was feeling worse, and the palliative medicine was losing its ability to palliate, he mentioned that sometimes people say they can't sleep and get prescriptions and don't take them and stockpile them until they have enough. He mentioned that sometimes a doctor can accidentally overdose a patient on morphine. But when it came down to it, he didn't. He couldn't. He said this in an uncharacteristically low voice, as if he were whispering, like he didn't want to let the words out.

She was shocked. "But why?"

She was so sure he would admit that yes, he had "helped" Arthur to die, and that then she would be furiously angry, relieved, grateful, angry. She knew he wasn't lying. She would be able to tell. The truth was, he had not helped Arthur to die.

"Why? Are you opposed to it?"

"No, no, of course I'm not."

"Then why..."

And why was she so angry? Not relieved, or grateful, just angry.

He said he wanted to tell her why, but he did not want it to "come out wrong." Come out wrong? Like mismatched socks out of the dryer?

"After that night in the hospital... when I saw you... I thought about you..."

"I know," she said. "Giving my husband a hand job. Turned you on." Deliberately crude, tough talk. "But what did that have to do with helping Arthur die?"

"I just wanted to be sure that I... was not being... unduly influenced... by my thoughts about you..."

"To do what? Did you think about freeing me? From Arthur? Did you want to?"

"Not consciously," he said.

"Unconsciously," she asked him.

"Well, if it was unconscious, I wouldn't have known about it," he said. "Would I?"

"How would I know?" Sally said. "How would I know?"

"At the very least, you have to understand that it is an

extremely difficult thing even without complications." His voice was more doctorly, now.

"I was a complication?"

"No. My feelings were the complication. I wanted to be sure that I was thinking of Arthur, his prospects, his chance of survival, his pain, the pain-to-come."

She had thought about this and thought about this. "Arthur would never have quit because of pain. He was too tough. As long as he could see me, see us, the family, and know us, and have a minute or a laugh or be with us, he would not ask you to help him die." In the interest of finding things out, she had decided on "help him die" instead of "kill him," though she was not sure which was correct.

Joe didn't talk for a long time. Then he said, "You're right. He wanted to die to spare you, the family, the pain. He said the 'new normal' – the routine, everything revolving around the hospital, his sickness – was costing you too much, in money, and in quality of life. He was afraid if it lasted too long, it would erase the old normal from your minds. He had thought about it a lot. He was firm and he was not afraid. At least not for himself."

"And you denied him?"

He shook his head. "I couldn't do it. If he had said he couldn't take the pain anymore... but he never said that. He said he couldn't take your pain. He was asking me to put you out of your misery, and I didn't have the right."

"Even though you say you cared about me?"

"Especially because I care about you."

She had imagined that he had killed Arthur, that somehow, he had talked Arthur into killing himself before his time. She understood that in the beginning, it had been a family suspicion, something to talk about to keep the question of his death open, as if it could make him live again. But then, when she got to know Joe, when she fell in love with him, when he told her he had thought about her, she was sure he had killed

Arthur because of her. And she promised herself, and feared, she would hate him for it. But now, it seemed, he had refused Arthur because of her.

"I love you," he said.

"I love you," she said. But she hated him, too.

"What does this mean?" he said.

"Nothing," she said. "We'll have to see." She was looking at him with a kind of x-ray vision, trying to see inside, to help her decide. At certain moments, of great anger, what it meant was that she wanted to kill him. She spit poison into his scotch, she cut his throat with her laser vision, skywriting die, die above his head as he slept. But even then, after the killing, she revived him, cradled him in her arms, breathing antidote into the story in the nick of time, because she loved him immoderately hard, harder than she hated him.

* * *

Rita was in the hospital. She had the surgery which was going to fix the cancer this time for good. As always, she was optimistic. Why did this make Sally so mad? Was it because she could not help thinking "stupid," which then made her feel mean and guilty? Or was it because she was jealous of such stupidity that optimism was made up of?

It was magical thinking, Sally said. There was no reason to believe that the cancer would not come back again, as it had before.

Joe said she was wrong to feel that way. People get sick, people get well. If you accepted one, you had to accept the other. If you are superstitiously fearful, then you should be allowed to have a superstitious belief in magical healing.

"Why?"

"Why not?"

She and Joe had driven in from the country together, and she was early.

Rita was out of the room, having some test, but they said she wouldn't be long, and Sally should wait in her room.

There was a woman there, sitting in the easy chair by the window, reading a magazine. *Motor Home Monthly*. Now that's interesting, Sally thought. So when the woman looked up, Sally smiled. "Do you own a motor home?" she said, to get things started.

"I used to," the woman said. "Just sold it. Well, technically, I still own it, until next week, when we go to closing."

"It's like a house," Sally said.

"Kind of," the woman said. "I actually bought it from my daughter, just to bail her out. She was getting married and moving out of the country, and she couldn't get rid of it. I had no idea I would end up using it."

"Using it?" Sally said.

"Well, I bought the thing for almost nothing. And then I was broke, and my lease was up and I couldn't afford the rent raise my landlord was asking, so I said to myself, I'll move into the RV, just until I figure out what to do."

"That makes sense. It was a lucky thing you had it."

The woman nodded. "And then, I was looking through one of these magazines, my daughter had stacks of them in there, and they had a lot of classifieds, for people to work at different motor home parks, in exchange for the free space, hookup rentals, et cetera. So I wrote away to one of them."

"You did all this by yourself?"

The woman looks at her. "Sure. Why the heck not? I always wanted to travel. My husband was in the military and we moved around quite a lot. My first trip in the RV was to Arizona. That's where I picked up Chloe. My dog."

"Then I went to North Dakota, and I stayed there for quite a long time, almost a year. Hard in the wintertime, I gotta tell you. Met a lot of native Americans, they like to be called.

Lakota. Learned a lot. Hard life, some of them. Then I went to Tampa, because I was fed up with the cold, and I stayed there awhile. Then my kids were begging me to come home, and I had actually saved up a little, so I came back, sold the RV, and put a down payment on a condo near my other daughter."

"Wow. You're quite an independent woman."

The woman shrugged. "No sense being otherwise," she said. "I don't see anyone stepping up."

Rita came in. "I see you met my roommate," she said, looking at Sally, rolling her eyes.

"Oh, I thought you were a visitor," Sally said.

"No, she's having her second surgery tomorrow," Rita said.

"I'm confused," Sally said. "I thought you just came back from driving all over the country."

"I did," the woman said.

"But... if you had... I mean if you were in treatment... I don't want to pry... but..."

The woman smiled. "I know," she said. "It was a little like patting your head and rubbing your tummy at the same time, staying in treatment and traveling. Hard to do. But it can be done."

"How?" Rita said. Sally and Rita looked at each other.

"I got doctor's names, arranged ahead, built in some down time. It's not THAT hard."

"If you say so," Rita said, as if the woman's extreme courage was a bit much. Show-offish.

"Wow," Sally said. "Wow. You're inspiring."

To which Rita gives a raspberry.

"I see you're feeling better," Sally said to her sister-in-law.

"That's okay," the woman said, smiling and inclining her head toward Rita. "She's a pistol. I appreciate that. What'd they say?"

"Looks good," Rita said. "But I'm tired. Take my sister-in-law for a cup of coffee and let me get a catnap."

Sally had an hour to kill until she met Joe, so she let herself be taken for coffee with the interesting woman.

"What's interesting," the woman said, "is that all you girls can't see outside the box."

"Meaning what?" Sally said.

"Meaning Rita thinks I'm crazy. And your eyebrows went up when I said I traveled alone. What is so hard to understand?"

"Nothing. I understand. What interests me is even though I understand, I still live the rules I grew up with. A woman needs a man to pump gas, a widow wants a widower, grow old along with me, you're no one unless somebody loves you."

"Just sayings," the woman said. "Song titles."

"I'm beginning to see. But I'm not likely to change. Neither is Rita."

The woman slapped the table and the spoon jumped. "Exactly. So don't put me down."

"I don't."

"Rita does."

Sally shakes her head. "No, she is afraid of you, because you think so differently from the way she thinks. Afraid you'll prove her wrong, in some way."

"I won't," the woman said.

"Maybe you'll change me," Sally said. "Knowing about you will change me."

"I doubt it," the woman said. "And let me say this: if a nice guy came along, I wouldn't say no."

"In other words, you're not so different?"

"In other words, I do what I want to do."

I do what I want to do. Who had said this before?

* * *

So, the interesting woman became the latest inanimate thing Sally talked to. Of course, she could befriend the woman herself, talk to her live. But Sally had no desire to become her friend, have lunch dates, meet her for tea, it all seemed too much trouble. Yet the idea of her became something that settled with Sally, or unsettled her. She talked about it the next morning while she was taking a shower: the three of them, Showerhead, Sally, and Interesting Woman.

"How do you do it?" she said. "How do you stay unaffected by what people tell you you ought to feel, or ought to be?"

She never said she was unaffected by anything, Showerhead said.

She just does it anyway.

I take my lumps, Interesting Woman said.

"That's another thing," Sally said. "To go against everyone, and just hit the road while you are in the middle of cancer treatment... it's unbelievable."

What makes you think it was capital C cancer treatment? Maybe it was just a lumpectomy and all she had to do was check in to see that her stitches were healing. Maybe her doctor said it was good for her.

"Why didn't I think that? Why did I think the worst?" Sally said. "Why am I thinking the worst now?"

Chill, Sally, Showerhead said. You're not going crazy.

Well, she's not going sane, either, Interesting Woman said.

Then the water turned cold and Sally got out and dried off

Part III

Evening: Home Free

So, poised between love and hate, crazy and sane, Sally made her narrow way through the days and nights. Joe was not put off by her talking to inanimate objects and imaginary people. "I hallucinated once when I was an intern," he said. "I saw my dead father, eating supper in the break room."

Now what was she supposed to make of this? "Meaning crazy knows crazy? Crazy appreciates crazy?"

"No, meaning not everything out of the ordinary is crazy. There is more variety in life than you think. You can act in a hundred ways and still be okay. A thousand. A million."

(Here was the love part. He reassured her, calmed her, made her laugh. He reached a hand up inside of her, made her feel young, sexy, daring, excited. He made her feel.) But then it raised alarms and she thought, "too much, too much," and she backed away.

(Here was the hate part.) Being in this relationship made her more than usually distracted, besotted, euphoric and depressed. Moderation had always been her life raft, and she hung on as if otherwise she would drown. And this inevitably made her think of Artie, her Artie, her dear Artie, her dear dead Artie.

What bothers you? Showerhead asks. State your problem.

"He says he loves me too often, too much, too easily. Like it's nothing. Like it costs him nothing."

And that's a problem, how? Why does such a thing bother you? Shouldn't you like it?

"Men don't just say it like that. Unless they did something wrong. Or they're about to. An apology, birthday or anniversary, to accompany a gift."

You don't really believe that, do you?

Did she?

As a girl she liked the bad boys, the ones who pulled her hair so she had to push back, and tell them to get off of her. That tension cord, the push-pull was what attracted her to Artie, what she imputed to his dark, heavy eyebrows and penetrating eyes, and few words. She fantasized a high-priced, hard-to-handle Heathcliff. Surprise! Artie was just a man of few words. But by then she had fallen in love with him in the way girls fell in love in those days. That love was what remained of all the banked fires of her imagination, but it had been enough. Of course, it changed her, too. Having been loved thoroughly but moderately for so long, it was what felt right. And too much now was hard to take.

Too much love, too much sex, too much understanding – she was not used to it. Take it easy, Showerhead said. Take it as it comes. Hot, cold. Easy. He was too easy, like a rescue dog who wants to stay.

Yet he wasn't some floppy nobody. He was not easy about everything. He had opinions. He voiced them.

You couldn't make him your bitch even if you wanted to, Interesting Woman said. So, he doesn't dwell on 9/11. So what? "Life's too short," he said. "Why should I make myself feel bad?" he asked. In that way, he resembled Arthur.

Like men in general, Interesting Woman said.

And he thinks your red car obsession is ornamental, like a frilly bit of lace to show your soft side.

He said his sympathy basket was full. She couldn't shame him.

Did you say tame him? Showerhead said.

His ego was fully muscled. His arrogance was intact. Ahhhh. And thus, she covered the space between hating him because he was insensitive and loving him because he was strong minded, in the time it took to think it.

And then there was the thing about Arthur.

* * *

Rita was cured. They "got it all." Her prognosis was five out of five stars. Doctor endorsed. A sure thing. And she was deeply depressed.

"I don't get it," Sally said. "She's happy as a clam while she's sick, and as soon as she finds out she's going to live, she gets depressed."

It's an effort to start living again, Showerhead said. Like jumpstarting a dead engine. It sputters a little. Look at you.

Pick yourself up, dust yourself off, start all over again, Interesting Woman sang.

Joe said it was not uncommon. Often people have struggled so hard to come to terms with dying that it was almost anticlimactic to have to get themselves back in gear, back into thinking about saving for old age, or paying taxes, or figuring out difficult relationships. "But then, once they get through it, they brighten up."

* * *

May/June. Spring was beautiful upstate. The green was at its greenest, sparkling and bright, with none of the blue depths and shadows of summer. Joe's house had become familiar to Sally. She had come to like the almost-austere simplicity of his late wife's decor. Even outside, she liked what she called the "absentee-landlord" landscaping, which required very little care. Tall shrubs hugged the cedar siding. A small column of decorative green flanked the driveway and flagstone path to the door. All the lawn ever needed was occasional mowing, and Joe liked to do it himself. She was sitting on a bench on the front porch, reading and watching him mow. He stopped now and then, remaining still for a time, as if he might be listening to the sound of their mutual happiness. He had just stopped when Evan and his hugely pregnant wife, Wendy, arrived, and he stayed there, waiting to greet them. Evan practically threw himself out of the car shouting "Dad," and he went to Joe, embracing him, practically lifting him off his feet. Sally watched this with some bemusement, thinking, "Wow, you'd think they were separated for years instead of a few weeks," but quickly corrected for envy, thinking how unlikely it would be for any of her kids to greet her this way. After a moment, Joe hugged him back, glancing at Sally, looking almost sheepish. Did he know she was a little jealous?

Wendy, the wife, approached her slowly, as if with extreme caution. Which made Sally want to say "Boo!" and see if she jumped. "Come, sit down," she said, crisply, and patted the space beside her, and Wendy perched on the edge of the bench. "How about a glass of lemonade?"

"Some water would be fine," Wendy said, her voice thin and breathy.

It was an unseasonably hot day, and Sally was glad to get back into the cool darkness of the house. She filled a pitcher with ice water and another with lemonade and gave Wendy, who had followed her in, glasses to take out onto the back porch, where there was more shade. She put the tray down and sat down herself. "There's a plate with cookies on the counter," she told Wendy, who, looking a little surprised, went in to get them. She came back with the cookies and some napkins and little paper plates she had set up beside them. "Oh, good," Sally said. "I forgot to tell you napkins." Nothing like making someone feel useful to help her relax.

Once she had met Wendy, she saw that she was not the controlling bitch Joe had suggested she was, but an extremely shy woman, and probably afraid of both the Messinger men. She had told this to Joe, who thought for a moment and said Sally was probably right.

Sure enough, Wendy perked up now that they were collaborators in serving the afternoon snack. "Anything else?" she said.

"There's a bowl of fruit in the fridge," Sally said, "But let's let the men bring it out when they come."

Wendy was wearing a complicated linen outfit, the kind of modest, expensive maternity thing Sally's generation used to wear; her feet were red and swollen between the straps of her sandals. Sally got an extra pair of flip flops and Wendy put them on gratefully. If she were one of her daughters, Sally would insist she climb out of the whole outfit and put on one of Sally's big, roomy T-shirt dresses. By the time Joe and Evan joined them, Wendy had removed her jacket and was sitting with her feet up, telling Sally something funny about her last visit to the ob/gyn.

Joe looked pleased. Even Evan smiled. But something was not right. The two men looked guilty, like they had just had a talk. Did they get the Tay-Sachs test results? Sally asked. But no, they hadn't heard yet; it wasn't that.

Through the afternoon, her feeling persisted that something was off, something was wrong. After dinner, which was a barbecue with Evan manning the grill – after a small struggle with his father for the tongs – they sat on the porch and listened to far-off thunder and talked lazily about everything and nothing, and in the comfort of it, Sally finally began to feel easy again. They talked about 9/11. She told the story of the red car, and to her surprise, Evan said he understood why she was so anxious to know what had happened to it.

"Then tell me," she said. "Because your dad thinks I'm silly, and I don't even understand it, myself."

"It stands for everything," he said. "Before, during and after."

Well, of course, everyone knew that 9/11 had changed life for everyone. For example, raising their child after 9/11 was going to be different from raising any child before, Sally thought. But why a red car?

Then the porch lights went out. They looked inside. It was completely dark inside, too. "Power outage," Joe said. "It won't last long." But a few minutes later, it was still dark, the thunder got louder, and it began to rain lightly.

"Why don't you kids take off..." Joe said.

"Before it gets worse..." Sally said.

"No, that's okay. We'll wait," Evan said. "I want to make sure you guys will be all right."

What was this exaggerated concern about? Sally, who had the flashlight in her hand, swerved it quickly from her lap to Joe's face. He was sitting opposite, and just as she shined it on him, he shook his head at Evan. As if telling him no, not now. To keep mum about something. What was going on?

"Why wouldn't we be all right?" Sally said.

"No reason," Evan said. "Just..."

"We're old," Joe said.

Wendy said, "It's not your age, it's the..."

"Stop." Joe and Evan said at the same time.

"It's what? Stop what?" Sally said.

No one answered.

The darkness reverberated, like the last echo of a plucked string.

"All right, you two," Sally said, as if she had given in, or given up. "Whatever it is, we're fine. Not to worry. Take off. Go home."

And since the rain had begun to fall harder, Evan, after lighting a pair of lanterns and setting the phone alongside Sally, reluctantly agreed. "Wendy's tired," he said, as a final apology.

"I'm really not," Wendy said, "But let's leave these two. It's been a long day."

It was another hour before the power was restored, and then everything in the house came on at once: the dishwasher resumed, the television drama in progress, the de-humidifier, the thumping of the office fan on low, the hum of the air conditioner, and amidst all this noise Sally said quietly, "You'd better tell me. You've been working up to it since the first day."

"I'm sick," he said. "I have something."

"No." she said. It was not denial, but refusal. Let it not be cancer, she thinks. Because she has wished it on him. Let it not be Lou Gehrig's. Let it not be Huntington's Chorea. Because those were the worst diseases she could think of, and she had wished them on him, too. Because of Arthur. The only thing she has not wished on him was Alzheimer's, because that was hers.

"It's early. It's a mild form. It's under control."

"What?" she said.

"Parkinson's," he said.

The stopping – freezing – in the midst of mowing. The way he appeared to be in a reverie, sometimes, locked in thought, between one action and another. He had the diagnosis for more than a year. It was why he did not do surgery anymore. She didn't ask many questions, and she only half-listened to what he was telling her, in the same medical professional voice he might use were he talking of some patient. But he was speaking of himself. Her love. And she tried to hear what he was saying, while being distracted by the voice in her head which was also saying, "Now, we're even."

And then, just like that, the summer was gone and it was late August. In the country the days were warm and gorgeous, moody blue-green, and the nights were cool. In the city, on Sally's block, people start putting flags on their porches and their cars, as they had done right after it happened, almost a year ago.

"Another motorcade," Mark said, as a neighbor rode by with two flags flying from the side windows of his late model Camry. Sally smiled. Mark had been hanging out with her, waiting to take CJ, who had been house sitting for Sally most of the summer, back to school this morning. After her love crisis she had settled into school more happily, and had lately been seeing a quiet young man, unlikely candidate for her stirred up young passion, who was a math major and wanted to be an actuary. Risk management. Probabilities. (Imagine!) They had lively discussions about Ken Feinberg, the man who figured out which victim's relatives get how much money, based on the projection of the victim's future earnings and probable worth. They thought he was awesome. They were Ken Feinberg groupies. CJ was happy. And somehow, Sally had gotten credit for this turnaround in her granddaughter's life, so since it happened, Mark had been treating her like a queen.

A patient of Joe's was a first responder. He took Joe and Sally downtown, to see what was there. It had become a tourist attraction, but not even New Yorkers made fun of that, and in a mood of generosity, everyone assumed no one was gawking. Still, Sally looked away from the vendors outside the subway stairs, selling T-shirts and flag pins and flags. She didn't want to know it. Joe's guy took them to a platform built especially for first responders. It was a makeshift structure, right near St. Paul's Church, that provided the best view of the pile of steel, rocks, and a small, cleared area of progress, ringed by a caravan of tractors and big rigs. It was a privileged vantage point, the front-row orchestra of the site. Sally listened to him telling Joe about the way first responders dug for body parts, and then she turned him off and looked at the pictures tacked all over on street light poles and telephone poles, and walls, of people missing and dead. They were blowing out candles, hugging Labrador retrievers, getting married; everyone living life in the pictures. She eventually looked past the pictures and tried to see over the wide clearing of ruins, beyond the tractors to where she might have walked once, but she didn't recognize anything.

It had been almost a year since the tragedy occurred, and things were settling down and becoming institutionalized. Everything had acquired a name. "First responder" was the shorthand everyone now knew, for firefighters, cops, EMTs, and had been expanded to include metalworkers, and the whatyamacallits, people who break up rubble. "Ground Zero" was what they called the place where the Twin Towers stood, in the WTC, which everyone knew meant World Trade

Center. Ground Zero was also called "the pile." "Survivors" were of course survivors, while "the Families" were those who survived the people who had not survived. "North Tower" and "South Tower" were talked about familiarly. Everyone knew that though the North Tower was hit first, the South Tower collapsed first, because of where the plane hit. People jumping out of windows was the hallmark of this disaster, the horror of horrors, the way floating baby shoes is to a tsunami. Air quality, affected by "toxic dust" has become political, and someone was suing someone over misinforming the public by saying it was safe to breathe. The Patriot Act, which Sally could not hold in her head for ten minutes and had to keep looking up the meaning of, was passed by a blustering, frightened Congress, and meanwhile some irrelevant and utter craziness set in: nuts were sending envelopes of anthrax in the mail to people they had something against.

When the towers fell, Sally had wanted to go to the memorial in Yankee Stadium. She had told everyone she was going. She had meant to go: cleared the day, put out her clothes, showered and dressed, locked the front door, got into the car and drove to the corner. Then she had turned around and come back, thinking, *the older I get the less I have to lose, and the more frightened I get of losing it.* Yet she had always felt that she was an activist at heart. It was just that *her* cause had never come along. Now, it seemed, that it had, though whether it was the red car – should she have pinned a picture of it on the lamppost? – or love and death was unclear. Whatever it was, she was not afraid of crowds anymore.

She was mortally sure – she liked this phrase and repeated it several times – she would not die in a crowd situation. She would instead die, in one way or another, of Alzheimer's disease. She had been assured that she was in the early, early, early stages, and that would not happen for a long, long, long, long time. That was three earlies and four longs.

Life went on. Alzheimer's had been diagnosed. Parkinson's

had been revealed. It was too much to take in, too much to believe. You couldn't get people to believe such a thing could happen. But it did. And it does. But then, for balance, Tay Sachs was averted, and Evan and Wendy waited more happily for their baby to be born.

Alzheimer's (if that was what it was – because one cannot really be sure with the tests they have now), turned out to be like everything else: terrible, better than expected, not too bad, frustrating. There were good days and less good days. No bad days, so far.

Joe was on one of a myriad of new drug options for Parkinson's, and was "tolerating it well." Sally was learning doctor's jargon, but tried not to use it unless she put finger-quotes around the phrases (and sometimes she forgot the phrase in mid-speak).

Now that the summer was over, she and Joe were back in the city, going to the country for long weekends, and only when they felt like it. Joe had decided to sell his city apartment, but Mark talked him out of it, saying he ought to keep it, so that Evan and Wendy could come to the city and have a place to stay. Sally wondered whether there was some hidden self-interest in Mark's advice, but for once, she kept her thoughts quiet. In general, her "domesticational" wisdom was getting lost in the underbrush of her new life... maybe love, maybe Alzheimer's, maybe all of it. In the occasional dropping of word or thought, the wild idea came to her that wordlessness could also be a choice. She no longer had utter faith in her mottos, aphorisms, comfortable saws and sayings. She had become an apostate. But it was in words that she expressed her apostasy, after all. Words are not acts rung true. Yet, "Brainstorms become intentions only by putting them into words" was also true.

And if she was going to start slowly losing her language, she had better start shoring up what would remain. A collection. A lexicon. She wrote down words to keep them alive in her life. In case she needed them. What words would she have to keep, to insure she could make herself understood? Because who knew what profound and world-changing thoughts still occured in her old brain?

Anxiety... She remembered when saying you were "anxious" meant you couldn't wait for something to happen. Now it almost never meant that. It meant you were nervous about it, not looking forward. Europe in the 1920s was called the Age of Anxiety. She looked it up. Now she called these days the Anxiety of Age. She would also be happy to forget the following words: ageist, senior, senior citizen, and elder (which sounded vaguely tribal). She did not mind "old."

She thought her collection of words would be alphabetical, but that was not how the words came. "Old" led her to think of words that were not used anymore, like "shirtwaist" which was once a word for a blouse, and "petticoat." She said "Ditto" to CJ one day, who didn't know what it meant. Dittos were purple transfer sheets for making paper copies. Schools and offices had ditto machines which could be loaded with paper and a ditto sheet and hand-cranked to produce duplicates of a text. Carbon copies were used in the home with a typewriter. People still said, "he is a carbon copy of his father" without knowing what that meant.

"If you lost a thousand words tomorrow, you would be still be ahead of the game," Joe said.

Assisted Living was not something she cared to contemplate, so she intended to erase it from her memory quite soon. No one believed in the phrase itself. Take the word "assist," a little rat of a word, which tied up "help" in red tape and politeness. Rita was moving into her boyfriend Bob's Assisted Living community in New Jersey. It was run by a big hotel chain and it was expensive. Which made Rita thinks it would be good. Joe and Sally went out there to see it. They met Rita and Bob in the clean, pink and green lobby, like a gigantic Lily Pulitzer fever dream, with white garden trellises over the doorways, on which were pinned notices and bulletins of social life at The Avalonia Commons. Rita and Bob were holding hands. The girl at the front desk said to the girl at the phone console, "Aren't they cute?"

"As a button," Sally muttered.

Bob and Rita had decided to marry. Right after Rita's last chemo treatment. It was the kind of thing Sally might have made a snappy remark about in the past, but not now. There was something about working together on a project that brought people together, even if the project happened to be dying.

* * *

Joe and Sally talked about it. Getting older, getting infirm takes work. No joke.

"It's a comeuppance," she said. "Let's laugh."

"Comeuppance for what?"

"For thinking you're going to live forever, that you are central to the world continuing, even to your own world continuing."

He said no. He shook his head. He disagreed. "It's just the human condition. The human body, doing its thing. There's no gotcha involved. But we can laugh anyway."

For a moment she thought the headshake was part of his disease. She struggled to find the words to say something back, a response. While she was trying to think of the words, he froze in mid-step. They looked at each other and they laughed. Joe said, "Are we dead yet?"

One night, Sally heard someone outside, shouting, "Hey, hey, hey, hey." She looked at the clock. It was 3 a.m. and the voice sounded like a young man's. It did not sound like he was calling for help, and in any case the word was "hey" and not "help." It did not sound like indignation, or like someone being pushed, or someone trying to stop a fight, or someone interrupting an argument. It does not sound like someone calling after someone else, trying to catch up to them, or asking them to wait. It just sounded like a young man shouting out the word "hey" multiple times without urgency, at 3 a.m. on a calm night for no good reason. Joe was asleep and she did not want to wake him. It occurred to her that the shouts might be a lucid dream, a dream she was still in and now she knew she was in. It might be that the shouts happened in a dream which she had just come out of, not remembering she had awakened. But those ideas did not ring true, as the sounds of the young man's cries had. What if the shouts were pure imagination, an auditory hallucination? What if the shouts had come from her? She struggled to remember that misperception is not always cause for alarm. She had misperceived things from time to time throughout her whole life, so why should it be such a big deal now? Riding along the Expressway the other day, she passed a stretch of flat land, the ground covered in dry dirt the color of wholewheat bread, with tall, giraffe-like animals sitting on it as if on an odd, Long Island prairie; but almost immediately she realized that what she was seeing was totally impossible because there were no prairies on the service road of the L.I.E. They did not exist. And the tall giraffes were really those yellow things... she struggled for the word crane till she found it and put it on the construction site, where it belonged, where it sat now.

She told herself all kinds of crazy things happen all the time. The world is filled with crazy things. She told herself that that momentary veldt on the L.I.E was not a bad thing to see in her mind's eye for a moment. What she saw was not bad in itself. The main thing was not to be afraid.

She and Joe played a game of who could quote the stupidest platitudes about health and illness. "Don't count the days, make them count."

"What doesn't kill you makes you strong."

"Tomorrow is a new beginning."

"Once you choose hope, anything is possible."

"Tough times don't last, but tough people do."

"You're not getting older, you're getting better."

He made her promise not to look up either disease on any websites.

"If you want to know anything, ask me, and I'll tell you."

"Then you'll tell me only the good things," she said.

But he promised. He would only tell her the truth. And for the most part, she kept her promise, though despite her determination, she had an occasional lapse. She looked up Parkinson's to find out if there was a way she could help when Joe froze in mid-step or mid-action. It said the patient should think of a march, or count off in rhythm, and the rhythm would get him free and moving again. She did not look up Alzheimer's, but she read somewhere that an early sign of decline is a diminished or warped sense of smell. She went around sniffing like a terrier, and naming smells to check that her identification jibed with what others were smelling. They laughed about that, too. But sometimes she worried. "If this or that happens then I will know something something something, and if it doesn't happen, then I won't," she said. Showerhead said that doesn't make a lot of sense. Interesting Woman said leave her alone, she knows what she's thinking but it's inside her head today.

In bed one night, in the middle of intercourse, Joe froze. He was stuck inside her, still hard, but unable to move. "Uh oh," she said. Now what? Feet do your stuff? "Think of a march," she said, but he couldn't, he was frozen. And she couldn't think of a march, either. She was just blank. Frozen stiff and blank as chalk. Then the tune came, Duh duh. Duh duh duh da da da. and the tune reminded her it was "Bridge Over the River Kwai" and she began singing it, marching it with her whole body until the rhythm of it broke the freeze but they kept on marching anyway.

Blank and stiff, but not dead yet.

Another evening, she smelled something burning, and her heart sank, because she had already checked that she turned off the stove. Was this the moment? Was this the sign? Was she hallucinating smells? But then she saw smoke coming from the vicinity of the kitchen, and she found a small fire where the glowing stovetop burner had caught the edge of the dishtowel that had been lying too close to it, and the flames had moved on to the oven mitt and the paper towels. Joe was just arriving home from the hospital when the firemen were leaving.

"Well," he said, as he watched Sally happily cleaning the charred stovetop. "The good news is your nose is still working."

Not dead yet.

She tested her deductive reasoning: woman at the checkout counter of Stop & Shop with a sample size deodorant, a scrunchy and two hairclips. "She's going on a vacation to a beach," she whispered to Joe. A car passed with the vanity plate BYTE ME 1. "Dentist or Computer Tech, hotshot in his field," she said.

So, for a long time – but out of time – they found ways to love each other and prop each other up. Her disease progressed faster than his, but he was ten years older than she, and his still sharp intellect was masked by drooping head, and tremors, so that waiters called him "buddy" or "old fella" and then she told them to fuck themselves. She was losing white matter, but, as she had once read, the disease was like acid hitting a tea towel and there were places where the fabric held, and sometimes they were both fine.

The house in Queens was their ground zero. Because the children were educated, conscience stricken and loving, they decided to join together to care for Sally and Joe at home, no matter what it took. But it was Sally and Joe and their true love that got them through the worst. When Sally saw a huge black cat bearing down on her, she struggled to know that it could not be happening, it was not logical, and the black cat became Joe again, and her fear went away.

Sometimes Joe walked holding his two hands in front of him, one protecting the other from tremors, and it gave him a round-shouldered, apelike gait, and sometimes, when she was herself again, she took him by the hand, and said, "Come on old guy."

Sally had a waking dream. It was about 4 Mile Square, a historical event the date of which is very clearly 17/7/47 – in the dream someone argues that there is no seventeenth month, but she was clear: there was if she said there was, and on that seventeenth month of that seventh day of '47 – 4 miles square was destroyed, blown up by – thing. Just like 9/11, she said in the dream, to someone. "You never heard of 4 Mile Square? Look it up." In the dream it was raining. People ran from the rain. In the dream, she said, "Let's meet on the day of the – conflagration or celebration? – when we know what day that is going to be."

Eventually, she saw white wolves in a forest and was at home with them, as they came and went, one shift after another. And then there was a time when the huge black cat bore down on her and she could not logic it away, but she had the courage to let it come close, and it was gentler than all the white wolves.

Sally's Alzheimer's was the freedom from everything. In the end, not even intuition remained. Sensation was all: what was hot, what was cold, what was bright or dark, loud or soft. The touch on her skin, balm or burn, or the tongue of a gentle black cat. Home. Free.

The End

The Story of the Red Car Which Sally Never Knew

Bryan McKay was not a superstitious man, but ever since his brother-in-law convinced him to ditch the car, everything went wrong.

They were supposed to park it somewhere and then it would be gone. He would report it stolen and that would be that.

They parked it where they were supposed to and next day

it was still there. His brother-in-law said the guy who was supposed to boost it had the flu.

Ask him what should we do, leave it or take it and bring it back another time?

But then his brother-in-law had a gall bladder attack and went to the hospital and then in a freak flash of bad luck he died, and Bryan didn't have the phone number of the guy who was supposed to take care of it, or even his name and he didn't know what to do.

So he left the car there. But even though he tore off the registration sticker, the cops found the car and traced him through the VIN and he got notified.

The cops asked him why he didn't report it stolen and he lied and said he did and probably because of 9/11 they didn't follow up, they just said he should go get it.

So he figured he'd get it fixed up after all or give it to his nephew, since his brother-in-law died and the kid was sad.

But when he tried to start it, it turned out someone had pulled out the engine, right out of the car. It was an empty shell.

So all in all, because of the car, someone got the flu, Bryan's brother-in-law died of an exploding gall bladder, 9/11 happened, and Bryan had to end up paying to have the dead car towed. Sometimes Bryan thought that if someone in one of those storefronts where the car was parked had called the police, Bryan would have taken the car back right away, and his brother-in-law never would have gotten stressed out and his gall bladder would have calmed down and the whole thing would have reversed, like in the movies where the wind sucks itself back into calm, and the blown leaves flutter backwards up into the trees and onto the branches, and the dead awaken and their wounds are gone.

ROUNDFIRE
BOOKS

FICTION

Put simply, we publish great stories. Whether it's literary or
popular, a gentle tale or a pulsating thriller, the connecting theme
in all Roundfire fiction titles is that once you pick them up you
won't want to put them down.
If you have enjoyed this book, why not tell other readers by
posting a review on your preferred book site.

Recent bestsellers from Roundfire are:

The Bookseller's Sonnets
Andi Rosenthal

The Bookseller's Sonnets intertwines three love stories with a tale of religious identity and mystery spanning five hundred years and three countries.

Paperback: 978-1-84694-342-3 ebook: 978-184694-626-4

Birds of the Nile
An Egyptian Adventure

N.E. David

Ex-diplomat Michael Blake wanted a quiet birding trip up the Nile – he wasn't expecting a revolution.

Paperback: 978-1-78279-158-4 ebook: 978-1-78279-157-7

The Cause
Roderick Vincent

The second American Revolution will be a fire lit from an internal spark.

Paperback: 978-1-78279-763-0 ebook: 978-1-78279-762-3

Blood Profit$
The Lithium Conspiracy

J. Victor Tomaszek, James N. Patrick, Sr.

The blood of the many for the profits of the few… *Blood Profit$* will take you into the cigar-smoke-filled room where American policy and laws are really made.

Paperback: 978-1-78279-483-7 ebook: 978-1-78279-277-2

The Burden
A Family Saga
N.E. David
Frank will do anything to keep his mother and father apart. But he's carrying baggage – and it might just weigh him down ...
Paperback: 978-1-78279-936-8 ebook: 978-1-78279-937-5

Don't Drink and Fly
The Story of Bernice O'Hanlon: Part One
Cathie Devitt
Bernice is a witch living in Glasgow. She loses her way in her life and wanders off the beaten track looking for the garden of enlightenment.
Paperback: 978-1-78279-016-7 ebook: 978-1-78279-015-0

Gag
Melissa Unger
One rainy afternoon in a Brooklyn diner, Peter Howland punctures an egg with his fork. Repulsed, Peter pushes the plate away and never eats again.
Paperback: 978-1-78279-564-3 ebook: 978-1-78279-563-6

The Master Yeshua
The Undiscovered Gospel of Joseph
Joyce Luck
Jesus is not who you think he is. The year is 75 CE. Joseph ben Jude is frail and ailing, but he has a prophecy to fulfil ...
Paperback: 978-1-78279-974-0 ebook: 978-1-78279-975-7

On the Far Side, There's a Boy
Paula Coston
Martine Haslett, a thirty-something 1980s woman, plays hard on the fringes of the London drag club scene until one night which prompts her to sign up to a charity. She writes to a young Sri Lankan boy, with consequences far and long.
Paperback: 978-1-78279-574-2 ebook: 978-1-78279-573-5

Tuareg
Alberto Vazquez-Figueroa
With over 5 million copies sold worldwide, *Tuareg* is a classic adventure story from best-selling author Alberto Vazquez-Figueroa, about honour, revenge and a clash of cultures.
Paperback: 978-1-84694-192-4

Readers of ebooks can buy or view any of these bestsellers by clicking on the live link in the title. Most titles are published in paperback and as an ebook. Paperbacks are available in traditional bookshops. Both print and ebook formats are available online.

Find more titles and sign up to our readers' newsletter at
http://www.johnhuntpublishing.com/fiction

Follow us on Facebook at https://www.facebook.com/JHPfiction
and Twitter at https://twitter.com/JHPFiction